Discover

Discovering God on the Farm

A Collection of Short Devotionals

Louise Berrington

Discovering God on the Farm

Copyright © 2023 by Louise Berrington.

All rights reserved.

No part of this book may be reproduced in any form or by any electronic or mechanical means, including information storage and retrieval systems, without permission in writing from the author, except by a reviewer who may quote brief passages in a review.

Printed in the United States of America

ISBN: 9798854898607

1st Edition

Scriptures marked KJV are taken from the KING JAMES VERSION (KJV): KING JAMES VERSION, public domain.

Discovering God on the Farm

Table of Contents

Introduction: Discovering God on the Farm 7

Part One: Lessons from Early Memories 11
    Lesson One: On His Shoulders 12
    Lesson Two: My Sheep Know My Voice 16
    Lesson Three: Swinging on Grapevines 21
    Lesson Four: Cracking Open Rocks 26
    Lesson Five: Facing Your Fears 31
    Lesson Six: We are Grafted In 36

Part Two: Lessons Inside the Farmhouse 41
    Lesson Seven: God's Presence 42
    Lesson Eight: My Fairy Godmother 46
    Lesson Nine: The Cream of the Crop 52
    Lesson Ten: Under Pressure 57
    Lesson Eleven: My Broken Leg 62

Discovering God on the Farm

Part Three: Lessons as a Young Adult 68
   Lesson Twelve: Calamity Jane 69
   Lesson Thirteen: Heed the Warning 74
   Lesson Fourteen: Too Much of a Good Thing 79
   Lesson Fifteen: The Scent of Lilacs 84

Part Four: Lessons from Nature 90
   Lesson Sixteen: Those Are My Peppers 91
   Lesson Seventeen: Flow Like a River 98
   Lesson Eighteen: Let God Plan Your Picnic 103
   Lesson Nineteen: The Necessity of Change 108
   Lesson Twenty: Keep the Fire Burning 114
   Lesson Tweny-One: Harvesting Nuts 119
   Lesson Twenty-Two: A Giver or a Taker 124

Part Five: He is Still Speaking 128
   Lesson Twenty-Three: Broken Pottery 129
   Lesson Twenty-Four: Hidden Sin 134
   Lesson Twenty-Five: My Ugly Oak Tree 138
   Lesson Twenty-Six: Praise Him in the Storm 143

Discovering God on the Farm

Dedication

This book is dedicated to the memory of my Father.
I'm so grateful for the love of farming he instilled in me.

Introduction

Discovering God on the Farm

Merriam-Webster - Definition of discover (verb): 1. to make known or visible 2. To obtain sight or knowledge of for the first time 3. To find out

I grew up in the country on a small 18-acre farm. My uncle had about 40 acres right across the street from us. He had the cows, the sheep, and the chickens. Our smaller farm provided plenty of space for beagles, a huge garden, a hay field, and a horse in later years.

My dad and his brother both had nine-to-five jobs outside of their homes but their real love was farming. And eventually their enthusiasm rubbed off on me. I find this old saying to be true, "You can take the girl out of the country, but you can't take the country out of the girl". I'm a farmer at heart. I love the great outdoors — always have!

Life was simpler in the 1950's — we didn't always lock our doors. There were seven of us children. We spent time outside, hanging out with the neighborhood kids, building forts in the woods, and ice skating on man-made turnpike ponds that weren't always completely frozen. We stayed outdoors till mom said we had to come in because it was too dark to see what we were doing.

Besides all the play time, we had plenty of chores to do. A big garden is so much work–planting, weeding, and harvesting. There was also lots to do to help raise the hay my uncle used to feed his cows. I learned firsthand at an early age that farming is not easy. And, amid many other variables it is completely dependent on the weather. The world calls it Mother Nature but I prefer to believe it is God who controls it all — the hot, the cold, the wind, and the rain.

In my younger years, I didn't really like the gardening part of the farm life. It took away from time spent in the woods climbing trees, playing baseball with all the neighborhood children, or just having fun outdoors. But that all changed when I grew up and got a chance to have my own garden. I found there was something satisfying about digging in the dirt and planting vegetables and flowers. It became exciting to watch things grow. It still never ceases to amaze me when a seed I put in the ground breaks through the dirt piled on it, turns into a plant, and produces fruit. Almost everywhere I've lived, I've always tried to have plenty of flowers and a garden of some sort. Once, I even had a really big one right next to my small produce stand.

Over the years, God has allowed me to *discover* who He is through the experiences I had growing up in the country. Some of these lessons took place in my youth both inside and outside of the farmhouse. At the time they happened I had no clue God was speaking to me. Later in life as I reflected on each incident, I realized the significance of what they revealed about my heavenly Father. I've had other experiences during my life, especially through nature, that clearly pointed to who God is. Many situations in my gardens caused me to take a deeper look within.

This isn't, by any means, a new concept. In the Bible the Lord forever spiritualized what happens in nature. Jesus painted easy to understand word pictures in His many parables—often referring to seed time and harvest. So, it's no surprise that He continues to teach us about life in the same manner today!

Just as the definition of "discover" states; on the farm God made Himself *known*—he became *visible* to me. I gained knowledge about Him through things He let me *see*. I hope you enjoy my stories as we stroll through my past experiences together. It has been a pleasure for me to look back and see how the Lord unfolded the truths of who He is simply by pointing out the lesson hidden inside of ordinary things that happened from my youth until the present day.

So, who is God to you? Has He revealed Himself to you? Maybe you don't think He has. I challenge you to look back at your life and dig a little deeper as you remember your journey. Discovering God is a process—but it's really not as complicated as it seems to be at times. He's not trying to hide from us. He's not playing some challenging game like Mahjong with so many difficult maneuvers that we can never quite learn about Him.

The God of the Bible made himself known so many times through natural things. The Father can be made visible by looking at the world around us. I am sure you will begin to see God in the many ordinary experiences you've had. In these few devotionals, I am going to share some of the unique ways God has revealed who He was to me.

For the invisible things of him from the creation of the world are clearly seen, being understood by the things that are made, even his eternal power and Godhead; so that they are without excuse:
(Romans 1:20 KJV)

The heavens declare the glory of God; and the firmament sheweth his handywork. Day unto day uttereth speech, and night unto night sheweth knowledge. There is no speech nor language, where their voice is not heard.
(Psalms 19:1-3 KJV)

Discovering God on the Farm

Part One

Lessons from Early Memories

1. On His Shoulders
2. My Sheep Know My Voice
3. Swinging on Grapevines
4. Cracking Open Rocks
5. Facing Your Fears
6. We are Grafted In

Lesson One

On His Shoulders

The Lord is my rock, and my fortress, and my deliverer; my God, my strength, in whom I will trust; my buckler, and the horn of my salvation, and my high tower.
(Psalm 18:2 KJV).

Everyone has favorite memories—those moments in time forever embedded in our minds. God taught me some precious truths about His character through some early experiences of mine. I was quite young when a few of them took place and didn't have a full understanding of the significance of the messages the Lord was sending until I was older. One of my earliest adventures was when I was somewhere between the age of three and four. This heartfelt true story has always remained at the top of my list as an unforgettable moment.

My family had a small orchard. Often, my dad would walk there to check on how everything was growing. This particular evening, he asked my mom, my older sister, and I to tag along for the stroll through the apple trees. As I clung to my father's hand, it was difficult to keep up with him — my stride was so small.

The tall grass frightened me. My father could just take a step and squash it as we went along. But my little footprints struggled to get through it. It looked like a jungle to me. My thoughts ran wild wondering what might be hiding in the grass. I was glad when I heard my dad say, "Everything looks great. Let's head back."

We'd only taken a few steps back towards the house when, suddenly, my father stopped. He looked down at me, grabbed me under my arms, and said, "Come on." Just that quickly, he swept me up on top of his shoulders. Immediately, my frown disappeared — I was grinning from ear to ear. There I was, safely nestled on top of the world looking down. Nothing could touch me. I'd been rescued from anything I'd imagined was lurking in the grass. I clung to him so tightly with my arms wrapped around his head.

My father had pity on his little girl trying to walk beside him. What I remember most about the experience was the feeling it gave me. No matter where life took me, I could close my eyes and flash back to how wonderful it felt to be lifted up — those gentle yet powerful hands easily placing me onto his shoulders. There is nothing quite like the certainty I had, knowing I was out of harm's way. This big strong man was my knight in shining armor — my protector. For that brief moment in time, I knew no evil could come near me; not as long as my father had me.

Later in life, when I turned to following the Lord in a more real way, I realized the Bible tells us all about how God shelters us. And that's exactly how I felt all those years ago —

safeguarded. When I read this verse, I was reminded of that day in the orchard. *He delivereth me from mine enemies: yea, thou liftest me up above those that rise up against me: thou hast delivered me from the violent man. (Psalm 18:48 KJV)* My father proved he cared by picking up his frightened little daughter and carrying her all the way home. And even though that was a long time ago, I can't help but smile each time I relive how he placed me on his shoulders.

We are God's children, walking with Him in His orchards down here. Sometimes we focus on looking at the jungles all around us. Life can be scary. We often forget our heavenly Father is holding our hand. My dad was well aware of my struggle to keep up. So also, the Lord is mindful of the fear that grips our hearts when situations we find ourselves in overwhelm us. He knows when the "weeds and briars" in life have become too tall for us to push through on our own.

If we are discouraged by whatever life may have put in front of us, we should pause and look up. It gives our heavenly Father great pleasure to place us on His shoulders. He not only carries us; He shields us as He fights off the attacks of our enemies.

Allow Him to be your "high tower". Let Him be the one to guide you to safety from a strategic position. Worries somehow fade into the background when you're raised up and looking down on a storm. As you read these encouraging scriptures, I pray they will help you turn your troubles over to Him. He has broad shoulders.

I will extol thee, O Lord; for thou hast lifted me up, and hast not made my foes to rejoice over me.
(Psalm 30:1 KJV)

Then they cry unto the Lord in their trouble, and he bringeth them out of their distresses. He maketh the storm a calm, so that the waves thereof are still. Then are they glad because they be quiet; so he bringeth them unto their desired haven.
(Psalm 107:28-30 KJV)

Lesson Two

My Sheep Know My Voice

And when he putteth forth his own sheep, he goeth before them, and the sheep follow him: for they know his voice. And a stranger will they not follow, but will flee from him: for they know not the voice of strangers.
(John 10:4-5 KJV)

When I was young, I'd heard the 23rd Psalm quoted in church on different occasions—usually at funerals. *"The Lord is my shepherd; I shall not want. He maketh me to lie down in green pastures: he leadeth me beside the still waters"* (Psalm 23:1-2 KJV). Because of the context in which I heard these words spoken, I usually associated them with death. Other than that, they didn't have much meaning to me. I certainly didn't know anyone who was a shepherd. Also, when I'd heard ministers say, "…my sheep know my voice," it didn't resonate with me either. Like I said, people weren't shepherds and I had no clue I was considered a sheep.

My aunt and uncle lived right across the street from us. My dad and his brother were part-time farmers but my uncle had all the animals—cows, chickens, and sheep. I never once thought of my family as shepherds—they were farmers.

It was exciting in the Spring when the sheep bore their young. There's nothing more adorable than a little lamb. Sometimes my aunt would put her flock out in her huge yard to graze. Of course, my brothers and sisters and I all wanted to get close to the precious young ones. We'd beg our mom to let us go see them. Whenever she gave in, we'd race across the road to my aunt's house. We giggled with excitement—each of us trying to be the first to reach them. But, instead of coming toward us, they scattered. All we wanted to do was pet them. No matter how hard we tried; they would never come near enough to let us touch them. After a few minutes, the sheep and their young ones were running all over the place.

It was then, my aunt would throw her hands up signaling us to stop. She'd motion us over as she shushed us. "Come here, children. Do exactly what I tell you. Stand very still, right by my side." With her finger pressed against her lips to silence us, she whispered, "You must be perfectly quiet."

We did as we were told and something amazing happened. Slowly, she began moving around her yard and talking to her sheep. As soon as she opened her mouth, they came running up to her with their young ones right beside them. They stayed as close to her as possible as long as she kept talking. It was easy to pet them when they surrounded her—each one pushing to get nearer to her.

Later in life, as I studied the Bible for myself, I read in the Book of John the verses with which I began this story. Immediately, I was reminded of the way my aunt merely had to speak for the sheep to come running. Her gentle voice meant safety for them. They knew her. We were the strangers as we called to the little lambs, trying to coax them to stop so we could pet them. They weren't familiar with our voices. We hadn't spent any time with them to earn their trust. The squeals of delight coming out of our mouths sounded threatening to them.

I've since learned a lot about how the shepherds worked long ago when the 23rd Psalm was written. They provided nourishment by finding green pastures, moving the flock around, and taking them to higher ground when food got scarce. The sheep rested in enclosures built especially for them. The shepherds slept nearby, usually lying across the openings to protect their flock from predators. They chased down any animal that attempted to make a meal out of one of their sheep. If one of their lambs was missing, they knew it because they counted them. The shepherds led them to still waters because rushing water could saturate their wool causing them to drown.

Jesus is our Shepherd. He isn't like a hired hand who runs when he sees trouble coming. Our enemy, the devil, is a wolf in sheep's clothing. The Lord has provided us with instructions to keep the one seeking to devour His children from infiltrating our pastures. As we read our Bibles, we will learn to distinguish God's voice. Take some time to stop and listen. Our protector may be calling us away from whomever and whatever looks harmless but is about to kill us.

And sometimes, we wander too far from safety and allow the enemy to get a grip on us. The watchful eye of the Lord knows when we've been lured away. We may have been tricked by the devil's clever disguise but he can't fool our

Shepherd. He keeps count and will come after us when we go missing. He willingly leaves the ninety-nine to find us. He's forever calling us home — searching so He can rescue us.

The way the Bible played out right before my eyes, back on the farm all those years ago was amazing. I witnessed God's Word come to life as those sheep responded to my aunt's voice. She'd fed them in green pastures and spent time with them. They trusted her because she'd kept them from all harm.

The old saying, "a picture is worth a thousand words," is so true. Now, every scripture about shepherds forever has a deeper meaning to me. As you read these verses, I hope they bring a better understanding about how much the Lord is looking out for you. Jesus cares! He is truly the Good Shepherd who literally laid His life down for His sheep. And yes, you are considered one of the sheep in His pasture!

I am the good shepherd, and know my sheep, and am known of mine. As the Father knoweth me, even so know I the Father: and I lay down my life for the sheep.
(John 10:14-15 KJV)

What man of you, having an hundred sheep, if he lose one of them, doth not leave the ninety and nine in the wilderness, and go after that which is lost, until he find it? And when he hath found it, he

layeth it on his shoulders, rejoicing.
(Luke 15:4-5 KJV)

You can find the 23rd Psalm printed out in the back of this book.

Lesson Three

Swinging on Grapevines

Let nothing be done through strife or vainglory; but in lowliness of mind let each esteem other better than themselves. Look not every man on his own things, but every man also on the things of others.
(Phil. 2:3-4 KJV)

Playing in the woods—it's what I did when I was young. My brothers, sisters, and I explored and built forts and treehouses. Spending time in nature was so much fun. It seems to be a lost art these days. Sadly, technology has been a big contributor to that. Many children today don't know the joy of having outdoor adventures. This was not the case when I was growing up. We spent as much time outside as possible. It was wonderful living in the country. But sometimes we'd argue over stuff when we were back in the woods—as we did on this particular day.

"I'm not trying it out. You go first!"

"No way! It's too high."

"I'm too heavy. You do it!"

"Come on, Joe! It'll hold you for sure—we promise. Here, take it and jump."

And so, the bickering went on and on. Which one of us kids would take the dare? We'd have to be brave enough to stand on top of the roots of a fallen tree, grab hold of a grapevine attached to something we couldn't see clearly, and swing across the huge hole those roots had left in the ground. None of us really wanted to be the crash dummy. We'd learned the hard way that not all grapevines were secure enough to hold our weight.

The woods we played in as children were a good distance from our house. You had to walk through two back fields to get there. So, no one wanted to risk getting hurt. Especially since an injury might have resulted in another punishment. Our parents didn't always sympathize with our shenanigans.

My brother reminded me the other day that he was usually the one we forced to be first to try out the vines. He was younger and we could talk him into almost anything. We'd swear it was safe but that wasn't always the case. We definitely weren't focused on putting the other guy's well-being first. Yes, we were self-centered when it came to many things when we were children.

We certainly never thought we were sinning. We were just kids having fun—playing in the woods. Volunteering to test the grapevine first never entered our minds. We gave no thought to valuing each other's safety above our own.

I'm sure some of us can probably think of a time or two when we've had this type of mindset as adults. But if we are really striving to be Christ-like, putting others' needs first should be automatic. It is not an option–it is mandatory.

Putting ourselves first is arrogant. Pride is that hidden sin. It's what's at the core of us wanting everything to be about "us".

A good example of one such prideful attitude is found in the eighteenth chapter of the Gospel of Luke. This parable relates how the Pharisee was thanking God that he was not like the evildoers. He spent his prayer time exalting himself — announcing all of the good he had done. But the other man, the tax collector, was so humble he wouldn't even look up. Instead, he proclaimed how unworthy he was. He prayed for God's mercy.

This short parable gives us something to think about. Self-examination is good for the soul. Here are some good questions to ask. Do I pray just to be seen? Do I exalt myself when praying? How do I view myself; do I think I am better than the next guy? Do I have a "holier than thou" attitude? If our answers were "yes" to any of these questions, perhaps it's time to take a long look at our hearts. Maybe some changes are overdue.

Start by thinking about meeting someone else's needs instead of always concentrating on how to make ourselves look or feel good. To stay humble, we need to develop that deep concern for others. These few simple steps might keep us from becoming conceited. First, let the other guy be in the spotlight. Next, always be willing to take the back seat. Finally, sincerely think about the sufferings or hard times someone is experiencing. As we learn to understand someone else's feelings and emotions, we will be better equipped to help them.

Another very familiar parable addressing our attitudes about caring is found in the tenth chapter of Luke. It's the story of The Good Samaritan. He willingly interrupted his own plans to be kind to a stranger. But he didn't stop after doing the bare minimum to help—he went above and beyond. Since he could not stay until the man recovered, he left enough money with the innkeeper to cover any ongoing expenses the injured man might have.

In the passages about the Good Samaritan the self-righteous priest ignored the plight of someone who was hurt. Turning the other cheek was just plain wrong. It made a statement—this person was not important. We definitely don't want to pattern our lives after that priest.

I always thought my siblings and I had fairly typical interactions with each other. Nevertheless, we should have been a little more thoughtful. Being a child wasn't exactly a legitimate excuse for being self-centered. Our trips to the woods could have been filled with less arguing if we'd had the concept of going out of our way for each other engrained in us from our youth. How much nicer it would've been for us to say, "I don't mind testing the grapevine. I'll go first."

Our journey in life will be more rewarding once we learn how to freely offer a helping hand. And not just for those in our natural families, but for strangers. Use common sense because there are instances when we do need to mind our own business. But, for the most part, there are plenty of times we should roll up our sleeves and ask, "What can I do to make a difference?"

Often times, we ignore a situation because we know it could get complicated to get involved. Even so, the right thing to do may very well be to put ourselves in someone else's shoes. We never know what extenuating circumstances may have put someone in the tough place they are in.

I challenge us all to think of a time when we've looked away. Maybe next time we can react differently! Whenever we are having difficulty putting the needs of others first, stop and think of the choice Jesus made for us. He freely gave His very life so we could have the chance to make heaven our home. Regardless of the pain and humiliation, He chose to accept His cross. He could have asked His Father to send legions of angels to rescue Him. He did not. We were His first and only consideration. Oh, to be more like Jesus!

We then that are strong ought to bear the infirmities of the weak, and not to please ourselves. Let every one of us please his neighbour for his good to edification. For even Christ pleased not himself; but, as it is written, The reproaches of them that reproached thee fell on me.
(Rom. 15:1-3 KJV)

Looking unto Jesus the author and finisher of our faith; who for the joy that was set before him endured the cross, despising the shame, and is set down at the right hand of the throne of God.
(Heb. 12:2 KJV)

You can find the parables in Luke printed out in the back of this book.

Lesson Four

Cracking Open Rocks

He hath made everything beautiful in his time: also he hath set the world in their heart, so that no man can find out the work that God maketh from the beginning to the end.
(Ecc. 3:11 KJV)

Growing up in the country with two brothers and four sisters was adventurous. Until I was much older, we were a one-car family. This meant we spent most of our time at home. It's different today. Back then mothers didn't run their children here, there, and everywhere. Instead, we found many ways to entertain ourselves. There was one particular thing we spent hours doing. I've never heard anyone else talk about this pastime but we loved what we called "cracking open rocks".

In the Spring when the back field was freshly plowed it brought lots of rocks to the surface. Gathering the bigger ones out of the field was a chore we had to do for our dad. It made the planting process easier. After removing them, we'd start our game of taking one large boulder and throwing it as hard as we could against another rock. We did this over and over until one of the rocks finally split open.

What we found inside was amazing. On the outside these dirty gray-looking rocks were ugly. But the inside — that was a whole different story. There were brilliant displays of glitter. The shiny veins of gold, silver, white, and pink were a sight to behold as they sparkled in the sun. We'd usually end up arguing over whose was the prettiest; not that there was any prize. It was an innocent sibling competition. We'd continue breaking open more rocks — searching for the best one.

We always showed off our gorgeous gems to any relatives or friends of our parents who happened to be visiting. Sometimes they would swear we found gold. One of my uncles often promised to take the pieces to the survey office for verification. We never heard back from him but we still loved the excitement of cracking open a plain old rock only to discover a thing of beauty inside.

And so it is with us. Unfortunately, we tend to look at the physical appearance of people. Some do not look so grand on the outside. So, we pass judgment on them based on how they look instead of stopping to consider that inside they may have a heart of gold. Today, there seems to be so much emphasis put on the external beauty of men and women. People invest a great deal of money making sure they look good on the outside but ignore their flawed attitudes and wrinkled personalities buried deep within.

Jesus had many harsh words for those who focused on what they looked like on the outside and not the inside. In the book of Matthew, the Lord addressed the scribes and Pharisees, calling them hypocrites and saying they looked like whitewashed tombs. In fact, the religious leaders did not recognize who Jesus was since He didn't come dressed in royal clothing. They missed it—failed to see Him as the Messiah they'd been longing for. They counted Him as a nobody just because He chose to come as a humble child born in a stable.

Where we are born should not label us. But it seems in our society today we still do just that. Being an American does not make us better than those who live outside the United States. As much as we'd like to think so—it isn't so. Things like titles, social status, and wealth continue to separate the elite from the rest.

Making determinations about others based on appearance only is not God's way. Unfortunately, some of our churches today don't accept some people as God's children just because of how they look. The circumstances of life may have covered someone with a layer of dirt until what is inside of them is unrecognizable. Regardless of how it happened, it is not our place to judge. If we would only learn to look beyond what seems apparent—dig a little deeper.

Let's take time today to reflect on how we treat others. The Christ-like thing to do is to look beneath the layer of hurts that has made many of those around us appear dull or gray. Some have an inner beauty which got buried because of the hand they were dealt in this life. Instead of assuming the worst, think about cracking open rocks. Help someone find what's hidden inside. Everyone has potential and beauty.

I did a little research on breaking open rocks. Some are called geodes, rounded rock formations containing crystals inside. There is a correct way to open them up. Certain tools can help to carefully chisel them, making a gentle score around the rock until it cracks open. It is not recommended that you slam one rock on another or use a sledge hammer. The rocks have precious cargo inside and being too rough will damage them—break them into small pieces which will have little or no value.

Likewise, as we attempt to spread the messages in the Gospels, the Bible is our gentle chisel to open up someone's heart. Instead, we sometimes hammer others using self-righteous words. Eventually, condemnation leaves them feeling like they have no worth. Once someone's spirit is broken it is not easy to convince them they have value. Remember, Jesus loves the unlovable.

I would encourage us to do a second-take when looking at those seemingly plain individuals around us. Many of us have passed by unshaven homeless men, standing on a street corner asking for food. Their clothes are dirty. If we've ever gotten close enough, they smell. Or there may be students we see walking to school. The ones without name-brand outfits, holes in their shoes, or merely dressed differently than us. Have we ever thought of who they might be underneath it all? Maybe they are a geode. Everyone has something inside that is precious in the Lord's sight. Try to envision those who do not look so pretty on the outside for who they might be on the inside.

If we can find a way to speak God's Word in the way He intended, we will begin to make those gentle scores around the outer layers of life that have made some appear dark. As we season what comes out of our mouths with love, we'll soon see those around us open up to reveal what they've been hiding within. When God brought the simple childhood game of cracking open rocks to my remembrance, He used it to teach me a lesson about the beauty within each of us—none excluded.

Throughout the Bible there are also multiple examples instructing us to be careful not to pass judgment on others because of how they look. Here are a few for us all to thoughtfully consider.

But the Lord said unto Samuel, Look not on his countenance, or on the height of his stature; because I have refused him: for the Lord seeth not as man seeth; for man looketh on the outward appearance, but the Lord looketh on the heart.
(1 Sam. 16:7 KJV)

My brethren, have not the faith of our Lord Jesus Christ, the Lord of glory, with respect of persons. For if there come unto your assembly a man with a gold ring, in goodly apparel, and there come in also a poor man in vile raiment; And ye have respect to him that weareth the gay clothing, and say unto him, Sit thou here in a good place; and say to the poor, Stand thou there, or sit here under my footstool: Are ye not then partial in yourselves, and are become judges of evil thoughts? Hearken, my beloved brethren, Hath not God chosen the poor of this world rich in faith, and heirs of the kingdom which he hath promised to them that love him?
(James 2:1-5 KJV)

You can find the scripture about the scribes and Pharisees printed in the back of this book.

Lesson Five

Facing Your Fears

There is no fear in love; but perfect love casteth out fear: because fear hath torment. He that feareth is not made perfect in love.
(1 John 4:18 KJV)

"**G**o out to the field and turn over the bales of hay today." It was one of the most dreaded things I could hear my dad tell my siblings and I to do. However, this was a necessary task since hay has to be completely dried out before being stored. Otherwise, it will mold. Our old-fashioned baler produced small round bales. A few days after my father did the initial baling, our job was to walk down the rows and kick each bale over so the bottom side could get dried out by the sun.

One of the things I hated about it was having to walk through the cow pasture to get to the back field. I was afraid of those gentle milk cows. To a little girl they seemed so huge as they swung their heads and slowly moved towards me.

But walking past the cows wasn't the scariest thing about pushing over the bales of hay. It's what happened when you rolled one over. It exposed the field mice who were setting up housekeeping under it. When their hiding place was disturbed, they would run out, scattering every which way. I would let out a scream every time! The thought of one running up my pant leg terrified me. Even though this was a chore we did in the heat of summer, I'd always wear knee socks under my jeans. I felt it was an extra layer of protection.

This whole fear of mice thing developed sometime in my early childhood days on the farm. Growing up in the country, we had our fair share of mice who found their way inside. It comes with the territory of living in a home built in the 1890's. You'd think I would have gotten used to seeing them. But I never did—they always frightened me. My mother never minded them. She'd set the traps. When she caught one, she'd just toss it out the back door. I thought it was her way of shaming our cats. It was their job to catch the little pests before they found their way inside.

I have no idea why I was so fearful of these tiny little creatures. Maybe it's the quick way they scurried around. If I saw one it sent me into panic mode. I guess what I suffered is more of a phobia because really—how much harm could a mouse do to a human? Some children even have them for pets. I'll never understand that!

Unfortunately, my insane fear of mice carried over into my adult life. It left me a prime target for being teased about my over-the-top reactions when I saw one. At the first sight of one, I am that person who stands on a chair screaming, "Somebody help me!" And I refuse to come down till I know it is safe.

When I worked at a bank the other gals in the office would sometimes place these fuzzy, fake mice in the drawers at my teller station. Over time, I knew they were fake. Still, every time I returned from lunch, pulled out my drawer, and saw one sitting there, I shrieked. They found my hollering out loud very entertaining. Even though they meant it in fun, it always left my heart pounding.

One of my sisters has sent me fake mice gifts for years. That tradition started after I'd had a melt down while on vacation at her house. Seeing one of the little critters run across the floor sent me into a tizzy.

This past summer, when I opened up my storage shed, I saw a mouse scamper towards the back wall looking for a place to hide. I'm ashamed to say I had to call a friend to set a trap. Then when the culprit was caught, I couldn't muster up enough courage to pick it up and throw it away — had to phone a friend again! I have got to stop this! I must get rid of the horrific fear that comes over me at the very thought of crossing paths with a mouse. I want Jesus to be the lifeline I call on when facing these creatures.

I started my recovery process by doing some research. This is what I discovered about fear. It can be good or bad. I'm glad I have the good kind — that reverential awe which leads to a healthy fear of God. The fear I need to get rid of is the one connected to the strong unpleasant emotion caused by anticipating danger. And in my case the dangers may not even exist. I am determined to find out how to be delivered from fear.

In my searching for answers, I found love to be deemed the opposite of fear. Love causes you to run towards something or someone you want. Fear causes you to run away from something or someone you do not want. Therefore, love is associated with faith and peace while fear is a comrade of uncertainty and anxiety.

The Bible has much to say about fear. I found it interesting that some websites said the Bible tells us to "fear not" 365 times. How convenient! I thought I could read a scripture a day for a whole year to help me learn why I shouldn't live in fear of mice. I certainly intended to find every one of those scriptures and begin to listen to what they said. As I continued to look on the web, I discovered that the number is not exactly true. But I did find plenty of "fear not" and "be not afraid" phrases in the King James version. I copied over 150 good references—enough to last me almost five months.

While reading over many of these verses, it became obvious that most people in the Bible who had fears turned to the Lord for their help. He was the answer for David in many of the Psalms. David understood his own weaknesses when faced with strong enemies. Putting those who were bigger than him or outnumbered him in the Lord's hands was his way out. He focused on trusting his mighty and powerful God to defeat his foes. We should do the same. Reading the Psalms is one way to help us put our faith in God.

Our fears are not always of things or people. An overwhelming crisis in our lives may make it appear as though there is no way out. Both in the Old and New Testaments, God's people were faced with many overwhelming problems. When such situations occurred, He spoke "fear not" to them. He did not condemn them for being afraid. Time after time, He made sure He let them know He would be with them. The Lord is already there is our darkest situation. He is able to lead us back to the light.

So, after all this studying, am I any less afraid of mice? Probably not! But it helped me recognize how God has gone before me in my battle. When I thought about it, I realized that even though I now live in an older home right across from a river, the Lord has been protecting me. He has sent many stray neighborhood cats who sit on my doorsteps or near the door of my shed keeping watch. The mouse I encountered recently was the first and only one I've seen in the five years I've lived here. I am so grateful the Lord will meet us right where we are at and work for us and with us as we learn to trust Him. Who knows? Maybe one day I will learn to take a deep breath when I see a mouse and trust the Lord to send the little fellow on his way.

What about you? Are you ready to face your fears? Remember our God is more than able to protect us no matter what the circumstances!

The Lord is my light and my salvation; whom shall I fear? the Lord is the strength of my life; of whom shall I be afraid?
(Psalm 27:1 KJV)

I sought the Lord, and he heard me, and delivered me from all my fears.
(Psalm 34:4 KJV)

Lesson Six

We are Grafted In

I am the vine, ye are the branches: He that abideth in me, and I in him, the same bringeth forth much fruit: for without me ye can do nothing.
(John 15:5 KJV)

I wasn't always a farmer at heart. When I was young, I loved spending time outside but wasn't that interested in gardening—it represented work. The fun part of being outdoors was taking walks to the woods where we built forts and swung on wild grapevines. But playtime sometimes took a back seat to helping our dad with planting or his other outdoor projects.

My father's love of farming got him involved with lots of different organizations. My brothers and sisters and I thought the name of the one club sounded odd—the Fruit and Nut Growers Association. Being silly children, we would laugh and say, "Dad is going to the *nut* meeting today." However funny we deemed the name of the group to be, my father learned a lot by being a member. He experimented with his different nut and apple trees and actually grafted branches from one nut or apple tree into the trunk of a different variety of the same.

My dad talked about what he was doing but it really wasn't important to me then. I remember how excited he got when the grafted-in branches showed signs of life. He was even more thrilled when they bore fruit.

As an adult, I came upon some scriptures in Romans, chapter 11. What a surprise—I saw the words "grafted in". The moment I read them the Lord took me back to the farm. He reminded me of my father's efforts—the hours he spent grafting a branch from one tree onto another tree. My dad would carefully watch it to make sure it took hold of the trunk.

Remembering this piqued my interest. I did some research on what grafting entails and why it is done. I found out it's really quite a process and was totally unaware it had so many benefits. Horticulturally, grafting is a technique used to join parts from two or more plants so that they appear to grow as a single unit. The upper part of a plant, known as the scion, grows on the root system or rootstock of another.

So spiritually speaking, we are the branches, the scions. Jesus is the vine, the rootstock. He spoke about us being one with Him as He was one with the Father. The purpose of being rooted and grounded in Him is to get us to operate as one with Him. We'll become a natural part of Him as we remain joined to the Lord.

Unfortunately, we aren't always a reflection of the one in whose image we are made. In fact, the multiple people, who make up the body of Christ, look quite different from one another. Even though we claim to have the same heavenly Father, we all have our own doctrines and our own rules. It sometimes seems like we've produced entirely too many variations of Christians.

Similarly, in nature, each seed coming from one fruit produces trees that do not look completely the same. This is one of the reasons grafting is so important. It allows farmers to reproduce exact replicas. What if we could accomplish similar results on this journey we call life? Wouldn't it be wonderful if those who belong to the Lord really began to look just like Him? Then, when the world saw us, it would see Jesus.

There are other reasons, in the spiritual sense, we might want to pay close attention to the grafting concept. The circulatory systems of the rootstock and that of the branch must link for it to survive. And so, with us. Staying attached to the true vine is crucial especially for those of us who are not Jewish by birth. We are referred to as Gentiles and therefore not considered natural heirs. But, being "grafted into Jesus" changes everything. We are adopted into His family and become part of the Lord's bloodline. As a result of tracing our roots back to Him, we inherit the privilege of walking and talking like we are royalty. Our Father is the King of Kings!

Farmers also graft because some varieties of trees bear better fruit while others have stronger root systems. Combining the two gives them the best of both worlds. The by-products can be more resistant to diseases and pests. So, I like to compare the plant diseases to sin. Staying attached to the Lord puts an end to the sins that keep us from producing healthy fruit. When we allow Jesus to accentuate our individual strengths, we'll be able to work together with Him to effectively resist the devil.

A grafted tree produces fruits much faster than a tree grown from seed. It also allows farmers to reproduce favorite plants with consistent characteristics. When Jesus really becomes our rootstock, we will produce good fruit quicker than we expected. And our actions will continually reflect the goodness of the Lord.

Grafting also enables trees to develop cold hardiness or water sensitivity. It gives them the ability to withstand rough conditions caused by sandy soils or by dry spells. There are times when the troubles of life make us feel like we are slipping away on sandy soil. The Lord will keep us grounded as we learn to be sensitive to His spirit. Being one with Him will help us stand in those spiritual seasons when our circumstances look dry and cold and dark. He remains right next to us as we navigate through rocky, narrow passageways. He is the light at the end of our tunnels.

I never realized grafting could bring about so many positive changes. It all fascinated me—especially learning about the ability to produce replicas. I've often heard this said about old married folks. Many think couples look alike after spending years together. Or you may know a twosome who think so much alike that they finish each other's sentences. If we would only allow the Lord to graft us in. Then, as we spend time with Him, we'll begin to look like, talk like, and act like Jesus. What a beautiful world it could be!

That they all may be one; as thou, Father, art in me, and I in thee, that they also may be one in us: that the world may believe that

thou hast sent me. And the glory which thou gavest me I have given them; that they may be one, even as we are one:
(John 17:21-22 KJV)

For if the firstfruit be holy, the lump is also holy: and if the root be holy, so are the branches. And if some of the branches be broken off, and thou, being a wild olive tree, wert grafted in among them, and with them partakest of the root and fatness of the olive tree; Boast not against the branches. But if thou boast, thou bearest not the root, but the root thee.
(Rom. 11:16-18 KJV)

Part Two

Lessons Inside the Farmhouse

7. God's Presence

8. My Fairy Godmother

9. Cream of the Crop

10. Under Pressure

11. My Broken Leg

Lesson Seven

God's Presence

Thou wilt shew me the path of life: in thy presence is fullness of joy; at thy right hand there are pleasures for evermore.
(Psalm 16:11 KJV)

When I was a child, I didn't really understand what God was all about even though my family went to church every Sunday. I was taught that Jesus died for me, but didn't quite grasp the concept of grace. I tried to make up for my mistakes. Most of my time was spent making feeble attempts to earn the favor of God. I distinctly remember in the weeks before Easter, I used to wonder why God had to prove He could die. And why was everyone so sad; some even cried during the Good Friday services. I would be thinking, *"Why are they so upset? He's not dead now!"*

Clearly, I had no idea the tears were tears of shame for our part in nailing Him to the cross. I blamed the Roman soldiers for that. Some of their tears were ones of gratitude for the price Jesus paid when He took our place on Calvary. It had never entered my mind that this was personal. At this point in my life developing a relationship with the Lord wasn't something I ever thought of doing. This is how I saw it; God was up there watching to see if I made a mistake. I was down here trying not to mess up.

I thought I loved the Lord and always wanted to please Him. But, my idea of the Heavenly Father was pretty much all about obeying someone who sat on a throne far away. Looking back, I realize, I served Him more out of fear—not love. If I followed all the rules, heaven would be my reward. The thought of hell frightened me—Jesus was my fire escape.

I had no clue I could actually talk to God and He, in turn, would answer me back. My prayers were memorized. When I recited them, they didn't come from my heart. Attending church and praying were obligations—not something I desired to spend time doing. Like I said, I certainly didn't want to end up in hell. Everything I did was based on acting religious. In the Bible, Jesus accused the scribes and Pharisees of doing just that—showing off how holy they were. But I didn't own a Bible, I had a missal.

My missal was a book with instructions about how to follow along with what was going on during church services. In the back of it were lots of prayers and some scriptures—mostly Psalms. Sometimes, I would go up to my bedroom and read those back pages. This was a room I shared with three other sisters. So, when everyone else was outside playing, I would sneak up there. It was a special time to be all by myself and say some prayers.

Being raised in a home with six other siblings, I'd always felt lost in the crowd. It was hard to get noticed or to be heard above everyone else's cries for attention. I loved those "alone" times. Whenever I was in that bedroom and opened up my missal to the back, something unusual happened. As I read the Psalms, an unexplainable peace surrounded me. It was so real and so heavy that I would just lay there—trying to be as still as I could. Eventually, I would stop reading, close my eyes, and soak it all in. I silently hoped this feeling would last forever.

When this first happened, I talked about it with my mother and some of my sisters. I challenged them to read the back of their missals. However, it was difficult to explain the kind of peace I felt. No one really understood what I was trying to tell them. Finally, I stopped sharing my experiences but continued to slip away as often as I could.

I will never forget how reading the Psalms refreshed me. I was on cloud nine after each of these episodes. To be honest, I did not even realize I was reading God's Word. I was not familiar with the Bible–didn't know it was for me. It was the big Holy Book the minister opened and read certain stories from on Sunday. Surely, it wasn't something I could read for myself.

Later in life, I had a spiritual awakening and accepted Jesus as my Savior. Finally, amazing grace made sense to me. It was then I recalled my encounters in my bedroom. Suddenly, in my spirit, an awareness of what happened all those years ago hit me. As a child, I'd had the privilege of sensing the actual presence of the Lord. When I realized that, it was all over but the shouting! Even though it took place long ago, the hush—the calm in the atmosphere of my room—it all came back to me. Only now, it was clear. God with us, Immanuel had meaning. Jesus was not just an imaginary figure. He was real and I could actually *feel* Him!

God is faithful and always pursuing us — creating unforgettable moments. He had allowed me to feel His spirit in a tangible way when I was young. At the time this transpired, I didn't understand how to know the Lord in a personal way. But I clearly remember the joy I felt lying on my bed — reading the Psalms. All these years later, it makes me smile just thinking about how He manifested His presence.

Today, even as I am writing this, I can feel a peace surrounding me. I want to close my eyes and let this stillness linger in the air for a while. You can discover this same serenity by searching God's Word until He shows up. When you feel the shift in the atmosphere around you — relax. Take your rest knowing He is right there by your side.

Repent ye therefore, and be converted, that your sins may be blotted out, when the times of refreshing shall come from the presence of the Lord.
(Acts 3:19 KJV)

And he said, My presence shall go with thee, and I will give thee rest. And he said unto him, If thy presence go not with me, carry us not up hence.
(Ex. 33:14-15 KJV)

Lesson Eight

My Fairy Godmother

But Jesus said, Suffer little children, and forbid them not, to come unto me: for of such is the kingdom of heaven.
(Matt. 19:14 KJV)

I was standing in the small playhouse—door shut, eyes closed, counting. "One, two, three, four….." I can't remember the exact number I had to reach before I would be whisked down to fairyland. It was hot that day inside the small shed. But I kept right on counting, hoping, and believing I would soon be there. I could hardly wait to arrive—it was going to be the best day ever.

You might be asking yourself why I was doing such a thing on a beautiful sunshiny day. Well let me tell you about it. My very own Fairy Godmother had paid me a visit early in the morning. It happened in my bedroom. She came the same way she always did. Just as I was waking up, I'd heard something in the tall wardrobe that served as the girls' closet in the bedroom four of us sisters shared. To my delight the door opened and she gracefully stepped into the room. She looked so beautiful in her real fur coat — it touched the floor. I loved to feel it and she never objected.

I was so happy she was there. I'd been worried about her ever coming back because on her last visit, I'd questioned something about her. It had seemed peculiar that her hair had been rolled up in those pink sponge rollers. So that particular day I'd looked at her and said, "Hey! Why do you have the same kind of rollers my older sister has?" Total silence for what seemed like forever. I was sure she could hear my heart beating.

Finally, she spoke, "Don't you know? Everybody uses this kind of roller — even Fairy Godmothers. We love putting our hair in curls." She then listened intently as I told her my wish, but promptly told me she couldn't grant it. My heart sank as she began to explain the reason. Permission for an outsider to visit fairyland was not something easily obtained. Those in charge of the other world were extremely cautious about who they allow in.

Weeks had gone by since I'd put in that request. I was fairly certain she wasn't going to return to me. After all, I'd clearly doubted she was real. She had every right to be upset. Besides, maybe it wasn't possible for such an insignificant person like me to enter into this world. Perhaps she'd let the fairies know how I questioned her and they'd never let me inside. My thoughts had been so unsettled after she'd left that day.

So naturally, today when I saw her, I was anxious to know if I was going to be allowed to enter into this imaginary world. Ever since she first described it — I could hardly think of anything else. I'd longed to go there. This fairyland she'd told me about was full of wonders and magic. It was real to me! So, despite my underlying concern of whether or not she was mad at me, I couldn't contain myself. Immediately, I started begging for an answer, "Well, what did they say? Please tell me! I can't wait another minute. Can I go to fairyland…can I?"

She was smiling as she spoke. "I had to do a lot of talking but they finally agreed to it. Yes, you are going!"

I was beyond excited. "Thank you, thank you, thank you! Yippee! I got my wish; I'm going to fairyland! Let's go!" I started running towards the door, looking for her to follow me.

Her smile had disappeared—she looked so serious. "Wait just a minute! It's not that simple. You have to listen very carefully to all my instructions." She gave me a short poem to speak and told me to count to a certain number. The place to stand was in the old small tool shed. My dad no longer used it so it had been claimed by my sisters and me—it was one of our playhouses. Of course, I did exactly what she told me to do. There I stood for hours, counting and hanging on to the hope of a visit to my fantasy world.

Needless to say, I never got to fairyland. It was frustrating to me. I wondered what I had done wrong. It left me feeling like I wasn't good enough—surely my fairy Godmother must still be angry with me. Maybe she hadn't forgiven me for questioning who she was.

Thinking about this incident from my past reminded me of the simple faith I possessed as a child. The kind of faith Jesus referred to when speaking about the children. He was never bothered by the young ones who wanted to be near Him.

Others tried to silence them but He invited them to come to Him. And He advised those around Him to learn from the little ones. In fact, Jesus told us to become as children in order to *see* the kingdom of heaven. I am sure it is even more beautiful than the best fairyland I ever imagined.

I've heard it said that God places what He wants us to be, in our hearts as children. I wonder if He also places those thoughts about an imaginary fairy-tale world inside of us too. Maybe He does so we will have no problem believing there really is a wonderful invisible world somewhere. Our human eyes may not be able to *see* it now but the Lord has promised us a home in heaven. And, we don't have to say a particular poem or count to a certain number to get there. It is much easier than following a lot of instructions like the ones I was given by my Fairy Godmother.

Looking back at my Fairy Godmother days made me grateful for God's plan for salvation. No matter how many rituals we perform or rules we follow we can never be perfect enough to enter this holy city in the sky. But we don't have to worry because we don't enter in because of our righteousness. We get there because of The Lord's goodness and mercy. God does not stay mad at us even though we have all questioned who He is at times in our lives. We enter in by trusting in Jesus who settled the score for us. He is able to permanently erase anything that might keep us from entering in. Simply ask Him to forgive you and consider it done!

Jesus actually holds the keys to this paradise we've all been promised. He went to hell to get those keys to this kingdom. But the price He paid to get them was great — it cost Him His life.

It's not complicated. All we have to do is acknowledge that Jesus is the one who conquered death, hell, and the grave and thank Him for what He did. He literally went to hell in our place and took the punishment we rightly deserve.

It almost sounds too good to be true! I know the old saying, *If it sounds too good to be true, it isn't.* But this is definitely an exception to the rule. The way to God's paradise is a gift to us. His son, Jesus, bought our tickets to this magical place. It's a home where there is no sickness or disease, no pain and suffering. A place where there is perfect peace—where the streets are paved with gold. We will live in mansions—they're being prepared for us.

As I get older, I want to be longing for my heavenly home. A place where I'll be surrounded by love because God is love. I am not saying I don't have love here. But I desire to have the right balance on my journey—to focus more on heavenly things than earthly pleasures. Some days I find myself wishing to be like that younger "me" who in my innocence and excitement could hardly wait to get to fairyland. I wonder if I am looking forward to my eternal home with the same kind of anticipation.

We are able to endure the trials and hardships we go through on this earth when we realize we have a future in a far better world than we could ever imagine. Yes, Jesus made a way for us to live happily-ever-after! Your ticket has already been bought and it's only a prayer away!

But as it is written, Eye hath not seen, nor ear heard, neither have entered into the heart of man, the things which God hath prepared for them that love him.
(1Cor. 2:9 KJV)

Verily I say unto you, Whosoever shall not receive the kingdom of God as a little child, he shall not enter therein. And he took them up in his arms, put his hands upon them, and blessed them.
(Mark 10:15-16 KJV)

You can find a prayer printed in the back of this book that will help you receive your ticket to heaven, the Lord's magical kingdom.

Lesson Nine

The Cream of the Crop

And the Lord shall make thee the head, and not the tail; and thou shalt be above only, and thou shalt not be beneath; if that thou hearken unto the commandments of the Lord thy God, which I command thee this day, to observe and to do them:
(Duet. 28:13 KJV)

When I was growing up, my uncle who lived across the street, had dairy cows. Our family was blessed with all the fresh milk we needed. They brought it over in a galvanized bucket—straight from the cow's udders to our door. Mom would tuck linen dish towels into the mouths of gallon jugs and pour. This process eliminated anything from the barn we didn't want to see floating in our milk. The jars were then put in the refrigerator to give the cream time to rise to the top.

The next day mom used a ladle to carefully skim the cream off the milk. She then had cream for coffee, recipes, or homemade butter. But I mostly got excited when she used it to make ice cream. Back in the 1950's there was a powder mix she bought for just that. I can't remember very much about it except it came in small boxes—like jello. The flavors were vanilla, strawberry, and my top choice—chocolate. She'd mix it up and put it in a container in the freezer. I could hardly wait for it to harden up. Wow! It was the best treat ever.

I loved the real thing—raw milk. I liked everything associated with it too—especially the ice cream. Also, mom used the milk to make dry cottage cheese—another favorite of mine. Whenever I visited a friend's house, I'd turn my nose up at their pasteurized, homogenized milk. Yuck—it tasted awful to me!

The cream is the best tasting part of the milk. Cream is what gives coffee or tea that extra flavor. Plus, it's where the vitamins are found. Fat-soluble vitamins are good for our bodies—they're healthy fats. Cream has more fat molecules than milk. As odd as it may seem, fat molecules are light. So, it's what makes the cream float to the top of the milk.

Remembering the cream reminded me how I miss that old-fashioned ice cream. It also made me think about God's people. Throughout the Bible, He wanted them to rise to the top. He called them to be separated from the rest of the people. Instead of listening, His chosen ones acted more like the heathens who lived around them. Many times, this was the underlying reason they were defeated by their enemies.

Unfortunately, we are fighting similar battles today. We are constantly challenged to change our way of thinking. Society pushes us to alter some of our moral standards. This made me wonder. Have we, as God's children, become homogenized Christians? Do we try to look and act like the crowd? Blending in never helps us get where we need to be.

And we certainly won't end up at the top by agreeing with all the latest fads. Sometimes in order to rise, we can't do what everyone else is doing. Popular opinion isn't always the best way to measure what is right.

Homogenized comes from the word homogeneous which means "of the same kind; of uniform structure or composition." So, what exactly happens when milk is homogenized? The milk is pushed through a membrane with force which makes the particles of cream very tiny. Therefore, they will not separate from the milk. Instead, they blend in. As I look around this crazy world of ours, I see many areas where the church has become a homogenized entity — compromising what they stand for and blending into the world's ways.

Then, I had to stop and ask myself if I'd become homogenized. I challenged myself to ask questions. "Am I afraid to push against the flow and rise above what "everyone" is accepting as normal behavior? If so, I must envision the Lord as being weak and small — unable to help me move forward when the crowd is going the opposite way. I hoped I would never forget how *Big* my God is!

Do I stand up for right no matter where I am?" My quest for an answer took me to Peter's story of denial. He was attempting to fit in as he warmed himself by the fire the evening the Lord was arrested. The scriptures in the book of Luke tell us he was following the Lord at a distance. The less time we spend with God the more separated from Him we become. Backing away from praying or reading the Bible makes the chance of compromising our faith greater. Eventually, as the gap between us widens, we will be too embarrassed to be associated with Him. As much as we think we'll never deny Him—what happened to Peter can happen to us.

A few verses before his denial, Peter swore he would follow the Lord even to the death—but read the story. Peer pressure in a public situation caused him to pretend to be one of those who was against Jesus. This is similar to what happens to the cream. To blend in it's heated, agitated, and pushed through a membrane under *pressure* until you can no longer see that it has different particles. It becomes homogeneous—the particles are the same as those in ordinary milk. Therefore, it cannot go anywhere. It can no longer rise to the top.

My advice is to never let our guard down—make every attempt to stay closely connected to Jesus. When the heat is put on our Christian values, we sometimes become agitated and allow ourselves to be pushed into accepting popular opinions. We become part of a worldly system and cannot separate from its standards. When this occurs, it becomes impossible to arise and be the beacon of light we are supposed to be. To do the work of the Lord, we cannot become a homogenized Christian.

It is time to rise up and be counted as a child of God. Be different, look different, act different. Otherwise, no one will recognize the Jesus in us. He is the cream of the crop—the best of the best!

Wherefore come out from among them, and be ye separate, saith the Lord, and touch not the unclean thing; and I will receive you. And will be a Father unto you, and ye shall be my sons and

daughters, saith the Lord Almighty.
(2 Cor. 6:17-18 KJV)

And it shall come to pass, if thou shalt hearken diligently unto the voice of the Lord thy God, to observe and to do all his commandments which I command thee this day, that the Lord thy God will set thee on high above all nations of the earth: And all these blessings shall come on thee, and overtake thee, if thou shalt hearken unto the voice of the Lord thy God.
(Duet. 28:1-2 KJV)

You can find the story of Peter's denial printed in the back of this book.

Lesson Ten

Under Pressure

These things I have spoken unto you, that in me ye might have peace. In the world ye shall have tribulation: but be of good cheer; I have overcome the world.
(John 16:33 KJV)

When reading these scriptures the other day, I noticed the footnotes in my Bible stated that the word "tribulation" is from the Greek word *thlipsis* which basically means pressure. Seeing the word "pressure" immediately sent me back to the days of my mother's pressure cooker. I grew up in the 1950's and 1960's. Microwaves were not available for household use until late in 1970. To prepare meals in a hurry, mom used this heavy-duty large pot with a pressure valve on the top. She often needed to throw a meal together quickly when she'd been shopping all day with her daughters.

My dad worked the day shift frequently. And, as old-fashioned as it sounds, back then a husband expected to have his supper on the table when he got home. We sat down at the table and ate together. We looked at each other—not a phone. We actually had conversations. Sad to say this is not how things are done today. Our busy lifestyles have eliminated our much-needed family time. But that's a whole other story.

Some of my mother's shopping excursions would get us home only about an hour before our dad was due to walk in the door after work. Those were the times my mother would shift into high gear giving instructions. Someone had to peel potatoes and carrots. Someone else chopped the onions and celery. We'd all scurry around the kitchen and as quick as a wink she would throw that roast with the vegetables, seasonings, and a little water into the cooker. Then the lid was twisted on—it had a rubber ring that sealed it tightly. That pressure valve was popped onto the top of the lid. The flame of our gas stove was turned way up—supper was on.

Mom always stayed in the kitchen watching and listening for that valve to start jiggling. Once the water inside started to boil, that regulator toggled back and forth to let the steam get out. The trick to that pressure cooker was knowing how much to lower the flame. It had to be turned down just enough to allow the steam to release at a slower pace. If the heat was kept too high excess pressure could build up and cause the cooker to explode. Too low was also a concern; it meant raw meat and potatoes.

So, mom carefully waited for the right sound—the slow jiggle. This meant everything was still cooking but with less pressure. About a half an hour later, she'd turn the burner off. After allowing the pot to cool down a bit, the valve was removed. Then the lid was twisted off. What was inside was a beautiful, tender, moist pot roast ready for the table just about the time dad opened the backdoor.

Pressure—we've all had times when we've felt pressed down by life's weary loads. Many of us have had seasons when we've reached the boiling point—we're ready to explode. Sometimes we think the Lord has signed off on us. That is never the case. God is paying attention, just like my mom did. He is always there to make adjustments when we feel trapped by the fiery trials of life. The Lord is well aware of all of our troubles and knows exactly when and how to take the heat off.

When adverse circumstances push us to the boiling point, we should stop and consider—everything serves a purpose. Navigating tough situations is a learning process—it matures us. The Lord understands just how much we can tolerate before we explode. He is alert and watching and listening as we go through difficult times.

I thought of three Hebrew children, who found themselves thrown into the fiery furnace. It wasn't because they had done wrong. In fact, it was quite the opposite—they'd refused to bow down to anyone but God. Remember, when the heaviness of our burdens seems to be pushing us under, it isn't necessarily a punishment—it may be a test of our faith.

The Bible tells us that the Lord was right there in the fire with them. The flames had no power to harm them. Jesus is also right here with us. With His help, we can make it through anything. When the pressure we are under is released, something good can be waiting on the other side. And if we look a little deeper, we may even be able to better understand the purpose of our trials.

It took a lot of pressure to get that roast to be soft enough to eat. Going through bad circumstances can prepare us to be ready to tenderly nourish and serve whomever the Lord sends our way. Enduring hardships is what gives us the extra compassion to reach out to those who are experiencing similar problems. When we have an attitude that reflects God's love and mercy, the messages we deliver will be able to offer hope to those who are searching for something to hang on to. Knowing we relate to their troubles makes it easier for others to "digest" what we have to share with them.

The Lord may also permit us to be in some uncomfortable spots because He wants to change us — get us ready for what may be ahead. With God's help we can discipline ourselves to concentrate on the positive results that are possible after our life seems to have been turned upside down. God desires to turn things around and work them out for our good.

Here are some scriptures to think about. They explain some of the after-effects of trials and tribulations. First, they help perfect us if we run towards the Lord when we're in the middle of a crisis. Second, they teach us how to help others get through difficult times. Someone somewhere is hurting. If you have the opportunity, I hope you reach out to that one who is looking to you. They need your encouragement!

My brethren, count it all joy when ye fall into divers temptations; Knowing this, that the trying of your faith worketh patience. But let patience have her perfect work, that ye may be perfect and entire, wanting nothing.
(James 1:2-4 KJV)

Discovering God on the Farm

Blessed be God, even the Father of our Lord Jesus Christ, the Father of mercies, and the God of all comfort; Who comforteth us in all our tribulation, that we may be able to comfort them which are in any trouble, by the comfort wherewith we ourselves are comforted of God.
(2 Cor. 1:3-4 KJV)

You can find the story of the three Hebrew children printed in the back of this book.

Lesson Eleven

My Broken Leg

Then he answered and spake unto me, saying, This is the word of the Lord unto Zerubbabel, saying, Not by might, nor by power, but by my spirit, saith the Lord of hosts.
(Zech. 4:6 KJV)

A long time ago, when I was in grade school, after lunch they sent us outdoors to play. In seventh grade, baseball was one of the favorite activities for the girls. It was a bright sunshiny day and I'd made it to second base. I wasn't really a very good hitter but I was a fast runner. The next batter hit the ball way into the outfield. Yes, I knew I could score the run. After touching on third, I saw someone standing right on the base line, but I made the dash for home plate. Before I knew what was happening, I was going down.

I heard a sound — like a crack as I was falling to the ground. I laid there screaming, refusing to get up. The school nurse was now beside me. As she rubbed my leg, she kept saying, "You're okay. It's just a charley horse. Please try to stand up."

"No," I cried. "It's broken! I heard it crack!"

After what seemed like a terribly long wait, the ambulance arrived. The paramedics carefully lifted me onto a stretcher. Lights flashing and siren blaring, we were off—racing to the hospital. Shortly after we got there, I was wheeled on a bed to the x-ray department. After taking lots of pictures, I was taken down to a room. My mom was there—dad was still at work. It was a relief to see a familiar face. She was so emotional; she cried when she first saw me. That made me cry—this had been quite an ordeal. And this was only the beginning of my miseries.

Finally, dad arrived. He would make any important decisions after he discussed my condition with the doctors. I could hear them as they explained everything to my parents. I was going to be staying in the hospital. The break was serious—my two main bones. If I'd listened to the nurse and stood up, they said my bone would have broken through my skin. That was a scary thought. This whole thing was scary to me. The thought of being put to sleep by an anesthetic was upsetting too.

My dad had always made us wear supportive shoes to prevent accidents like this from happening. I remember he was upset because I *did* have on my built-up saddle shoes but they didn't protect me from breaking my leg. Sometimes our best laid plans aren't enough to stop bad things from taking place. Life doesn't always go as we would like.

After the surgery, the pain was still there. This was all so overwhelming to me. I'd rarely spent the night away from home and I hated the hospital food. Plus, the cast was not small. It was this huge heavy plaster thing—covering my entire leg. It went from the very top of my upper thigh all the way down to my foot with only the tips of my toes still visible.

I couldn't even lift the big ugly thing! I remember being kind of snippy with my mother when she asked me how I felt. My response was so sarcastic. "Oh, I'm just fine!" Then I spoke sharply. "How do you think I feel? Look at my leg."

I hated everything about the situation I'd found myself in. But it was no excuse to be crabby—especially with my mother. I was so disrespectful and later was sorry about how I'd treated her.

Sometimes as adults we get irritable when we're physically sick. It's difficult to be nice when we aren't feeling well, particularly if we are suffering with a chronic condition. Sometimes we get nasty with our heavenly Father. We yell at Him instead of the real culprit. The devil is the one who came to steal, kill, and destroy. We should be shouting at Satan and using God's words to fight the devil.

I did other things I am not proud of as I navigated through this time of being semi-invalid. After some therapy, I was released from the hospital. But I still couldn't seem to be able to lift my leg with the heavy cast on it. So, me walking with crutches was quite the sight. If I remember correctly, I'd go backwards and try to drag my leg. Once I got home, I laid around and let my family wait on me. Everyone helped me do everything—and I liked it like that!

But then "the day" came. My dad was standing there, looking stern when he spoke. "You have to go back to school. The doctors say you should be able to lift your leg up by now. At least enough to use the crutches. You will be returning to school tomorrow." Telling my dad, you weren't going to do something, wasn't an option in our household.

Discovering God on the Farm

So, this is how it played out the next day. On the drive there my father informed me that I would be riding the bus home. Panic was setting in. I had no idea how I could even walk at school and he expected me to climb into a school bus. My thoughts were running wild. But, to my surprise when he helped me out of the car, something unusual happened. I lifted my leg off the ground, put my crutches under my arms, and went forward into the building. Everyone was watching and under pressure I made myself do what I should've been doing all along. I never put in the effort at home since I'd gotten used to being pampered.

Sometimes in life we settle into routines that seem to be good for us. We do what I did back then; we stay in our comfort zones because it's easy. We lock ourselves into being satisfied with doing the bare minimum. But if we'd just put forth the effort, we might be surprised at what we can accomplish. I didn't know I could lift my leg until I got out of the car the day I went back to school. In that moment I had no choice. When I gave it my all, it worked and I picked my heavy cast up. I was able to do what I'd convinced myself was impossible.

Incidentally, just because I was now able to properly walk on crutches, did not make me quit taking advantage of my handicap. Most evenings after supper, I would say my leg hurt. Mom would always tell me to go rest. She'd let my sisters clean up and do the dishes. My siblings saw right through my act. They paid me back by announcing they were going ice skating or snow-sled coasting. These were the things I had loved doing before my accident. I deserved their teasing since I continued to use every excuse to get out of helping around the house.

Thinking about this made me wonder. How many times have I tried to pretend I am handicapped to excuse myself from being obedient to whatever God has asked me to do? Maybe more times than I'm willing to admit. And after all these years I should know I can't fool Him. God will never ask us to do something He knows we can't do. Perhaps it's time for all of us to realize we aren't called to just ride along. Take that first step to lift the load we thought was too heavy. The Lord is able to make it easier than we ever imagined.

There are many examples in the Bible demonstrating how the Lord reacted when those He called gave their human weaknesses as a reason for not doing what He asked. Moses tried to say he couldn't speak well enough to talk to Pharaoh. God used him anyway! Gideon questioned his assignment to deliver his people out of the hands of the Midianites because his family was poor and insignificant. God miraculously gave him the victory with only a handful of men. Paul had a thorn in his flesh. Even though it wasn't removed, he remained faithful to his calling.

Life is not about trying to show how strong we are. God wants the world to see His power and might which become so apparent in the middle of our weaknesses. It is when we trust Him that all things become possible!

And the Lord looked upon him, and said, Go in this thy might, and thou shalt save Israel from the hand of the Midianites: have not I sent thee? And he said unto him, Oh my Lord, wherewith shall I save Israel? behold, my family is poor in Manasseh, and I am the least in my father's house. And the Lord said unto him, Surely I

will be with thee, and thou shalt smite the Midianites as one man.
(Judges 6:14-16 KJV)

And lest I should be exalted above measure through the abundance of the revelations, there was given to me a thorn in the flesh, the messenger of Satan to buffet me, lest I should be exalted above measure. For this thing I besought the Lord thrice, that it might depart from me. And he said unto me, My grace is sufficient for thee: for my strength is made perfect in weakness. Most gladly therefore will I rather glory in my infirmities, that the power of Christ may rest upon me.
(2 Cor. 12:7-9 KJV)

Part Three

Lessons as a Young Adult

12. Calamity Jane

13. Heed the Warning

14. Too Much of a Good Thing

15. The Scent of Lilacs

Lesson Twelve

Calamity Jane

Not that I speak in respect of want: for I have learned, in whatsoever state I am, therewith to be content.
(Phil. 4:11 KJV)

They say names have significance. Our horse's name was Calamity Jane and she owned it. One Saturday afternoon we lost our beloved mare in a tragic accident. It was hard to bear but there was something that made it even worse. It didn't have to happen. I went over the whole thing in my mind and questioned, *"Why did Jane, have to reach for the hay stacked on the other side of the wall? The huge bin at the front of her stall was full."* Her senseless act came with a great price — her life.

Outside our bedroom window we could hear the lonely whinny of her foal, Baby Jane. She was calling for her mother over and over and over. My brothers and sisters and I were also missing our family horse so much. Her baby's pitiful cries were beginning to wear on us. We knew, no matter how long this young filly called, it wouldn't bring her mother back —

Calamity Jane was gone forever. The sound of Baby Jane pining made us all start sobbing. And as our tears trickled down our cheeks, we all kept asking why. Why did Calamity do what she did?

The way the barn was set up was an underlying cause of our horse losing her life. My dad had built this solid wall which ran up to the rafters on the one side of our horse's stall. He did this because my mom was very timid around horses. Sometimes, when my siblings and I were in a hurry to catch the bus in the mornings, she'd offer to do the feeding. Other times she just wanted to give our horse a carrot or an apple. With the partition there, she could walk down the aisle, without any fear, and toss whatever she had into Jane's manger through this one small square window.

But the reason for this accident wasn't just the design of the barn. We will never understand why our horse decided to reach for the hay that was on the other side of the window. By doing so, she got her jowl caught in that small opening and panicked. We heard her squeals as she thrashed to get free. Her feet had slid under her so she was unable to stand up.

We ran to the barn and tried to knock out the wall but to no avail. The boys next door heard us yelling as we pounded on the hard barrier. They rushed over to help but weren't fast enough to round up some tools to break down the wall. By the time they freed her it was too late—she'd collapsed and died. Oh, how we all wept over her. It made no sense—she died trying to reach for something she already had.

Thinking about this incident from a long time ago made me ask some questions. Do we have a table spread before us with everything we need and yet try to look for something we think might be better? Do we stretch our necks trying to reach for what the neighbors seem to have? Why do other's blessings look better to us than what is right in front of us? If we get so busy looking at what we don't have, we may fail to see what is right under our noses. The hay on the other side of the wall was the same hay as was in Jane's trough already. As the old saying goes, the grass is not really greener on the other side of the fence.

Greed is a terrible thing. Seeking more and more is a self-centered mind set. Truthfully, having much is not what satisfies the soul. Contentment comes from having a relationship with the one who gives all gifts — the Lord. When we trust Him to sustain us, we will not always have to *see* the provisions. Our faith gives us the confidence to know that whatever we need will be supplied at the right time.

Having something saved for a rainy day isn't wrong, unless we believe our nest egg is all we have to fall back on. Amassing material possessions sometimes gives a false sense of security. What we own is not to be used as a safety cushion. Our hope and trust should remain in the Lord.

It's okay to have nice things. But when we become obsessed with wanting more, those things we acquire can become our idols. The Bible tells us we cannot serve two masters. God alone deserves first place in our hearts. Be careful not to allow having an abundance of whatever gives us security, cause us to put God on the shelf. We never cease to need the Lord.

Desiring something we really don't need can have tragic results and far-reaching effects. Because of Jane's attempt to get something she already had, everyone else had to suffer.

Discovering God on the Farm

Our Baby Jane had to be weaned earlier than expected. She would whinny and cry for her mother for days. We all were going to miss the good times we had with our horse — most of us enjoyed riding. Those were the consequences for her wrong choice. The cost of getting more than enough led her into a tight spot — one she couldn't back out of.

Often, we think more will help when it can actually make things worse. We should make sure we are reaching for only what was intended for us — nothing more — nothing less! Think twice before we extend our hand — asking for more. Remember what happened to Calamity Jane!

Paul instructs us in his epistles to be content with what we have. There is no time like the present to look carefully at the provisions the Lord has set before us and be thankful for them. I intend to be intentional about seeing what I already have. Then I want to be sure my happiness is not dependent on how much I own.

And, the Lord really is the solution to getting over the dilemma of never having enough. When we fix our eyes on eternal things instead of material things, we store up treasures in heaven. We will no longer desire the riches of this world. The Bible tells us that all we have need of, God's hand provides. What a wonderful promise! I hope we will always be appreciative of the blessings of the Lord. When we maintain this kind of a godly attitude, we will see our glasses as half full — not half empty. Praying we all have grateful hearts today!

Discovering God on the Farm

But godliness with contentment is great gain. [7] For we brought nothing into this world, and it is certain we can carry nothing out. [8] And having food and raiment let us be therewith content.
(1 Tim. 6:6-9 KJV)

Therefore take no thought, saying, What shall we eat? or, What shall we drink? or, Wherewithal shall we be clothed? [32] (For after all these things do the Gentiles seek:) for your heavenly Father knoweth that ye have need of all these things. [33] But seek ye first the kingdom of God, and his righteousness; and all these things shall be added unto you.
(Matt. 6:31-33 KJV)

Lesson Thirteen

Heed the Warning

Enter not into the path of the wicked, and go not in the way of evil men. Avoid it, pass not by it, turn from it, and pass away.
(Prov. 4:14-15 KJV)

After my father-in-law passed away, my husband and I inherited his German Shepherd, Heidi. She was a large, powerful dog who was intimidating to say the least. Her bark was enough to send the bravest of the brave running. And she was definitely overly protective of her family.

We never had to be afraid of her. She'd never bite the hand of the one's who fed her. We cared about her. She liked us. It was part of Heidi's personality—if she liked you, she liked you. But, if she didn't, you'd better warn us if you were coming to visit. Strangers waited in their cars if she was roaming about the yard when they pulled in our driveway. Some who ventured out despite her ferocious barking, found themselves praying to make it back to the safety of their vehicles.

Discovering God on the Farm

Heidi was mostly an outside dog who was left to run free during the day when we were home. At other times she was kept on a long chain attached to her big dog house which was next to the garage. She could also go in and out of the garage. It had plenty of space where she could find shelter from bad weather. During the cold winter months, especially as she got older, we'd bring her inside. We also always allowed her in during thunderstorms. She was petrified of the loud thunder and flashes of lightning. In her later years, a lot of commotion and noise of any kind irritated her. This brings me to my story about listening to warnings.

It was a lovely day outside. I was grateful because all the girls who were attending my daughter's birthday party could be noisy outdoors. As an extra precaution I put Heidi inside the horse barn chaining her to one of the stall doors. Specific instructions were given to everyone to stay out of the barn — away from the dog. It was a warm day in June so the big barn doors were left open so the breeze could blow through. That helped keep it cool in there. After lecturing everyone about how vicious our dog was, I assumed it was settled.

I went inside to gather together the food and games. This was going to be a fun day. As I was carrying a load of things out to the backyard, I saw my daughter and her friends chasing each other–laughing and screaming. To my dismay, they were going in one barn door and coming out the other — the exact thing I'd asked them not to do. I could hear Heidi barking loudly as screeching girls ran past her. This had to stop! Before I had time to get to the barn, my daughter came running out screaming, "Heidi has Megan!"

My heart skipped a beat as I raced into the barn. It was a horrible scene — the dog had Megan pinned up against a stall door. Her arm was in Heidi's mouth. I don't know how but I was able to get our dog to let go. It had to be God! The blood was pouring out of the wound. We hurried the young girl into the house and wrapped her arm tightly. After a quick call to her mother, we were off to the hospital—this was going to need stitches.

Facing Megan's mother was very difficult for me. It would sound ridiculous if I tried to explain how I'd warned the girls. This was not the time for excuses—the injury was going to leave a scar on her daughter's arm. There wasn't anything I could say to change that.

The meeting in the hospital turned out to be pleasant enough with no angry outbursts or accusations about whose fault it was. Megan's very concerned mother was obviously only interested in comforting her daughter. Lots of stitches were needed. We all went home with heavy hearts. Eventually, the wound healed and the family never once mentioned retaliation. There had been that unspoken threat of a lawsuit that hung over our heads for a while.

Today, thinking about this incident brought me to look deep within. Sometimes the Lord may ask us to stay away from certain people. He knows us better than we know ourselves—knows who may be a dangerous influence. In His Word, God explains the risks involved if we hang out with those He's warned us about. He's well aware our human nature is weak. So, do we always listen and stay away from those who might pull us in the wrong direction? Not really! Just because He said so doesn't always deter us.

It seems as though many of us are swayed by what everyone else is doing. We tend to follow the crowd. Other times we simply think we know better; especially when we're young. It looks like those in the world around us are having some harmless fun—doing whatever they want—running free.

The girls at my daughter's party got caught up in the moment of having a good time and totally forgot the warning. And sometimes so do we. The next thing we know, it's too late—the enemy has our back against the wall. He has a grip on us. But God, thankfully, has our back. One word from the Lord and the devil has to let go. God is a God of mercy. He understands the "why" behind the decisions we've made. Unfortunately, some of the messes we create leave scars and some scars are permanent.

The Bible is here to help us on our journey. I think we would be wise to allow ourselves to be guided by the scriptures that advise us whom to avoid. Over and over, the Lord says He will be with us if we heed His words. We can save ourselves some heartbreak if we pay attention to His warnings.

I had the girls' best interests at heart when I told them not to go near the dog. God cares so much that He left us an entire book full of instructions about whom we should fellowship with—or avoid. Take some time today to evaluate with whom you surround yourself. Are those you associate with lifting you up or pulling you down? Are they bringing you closer to the Lord or drawing you farther away from Him? May your inner circle of friends be the ones God has chosen for you.

Now we command you, brethren, in the name of our Lord Jesus Christ, that ye withdraw yourselves from every brother that walketh disorderly, and not after the tradition which he received of us. For yourselves know how ye ought to follow us: for we behaved not ourselves disorderly among you;
(2 Thess. 3:6-7 KJV)

Blessed is the man that walketh not in the counsel of the ungodly, nor standeth in the way of sinners, nor sitteth in the seat of the scornful. But his delight is in the law of the Lord; and in his law doth he meditate day and night.
(Psalm 1:1-2 KJV)

Discovering God on the Farm

Lesson Fourteen

Too Much of a Good Thing

For I bear them record that they have a zeal of God, but not according to knowledge. For they being ignorant of God's righteousness, and going about to establish their own righteousness, have not submitted themselves unto the righteousness of God.
(Rom. 10:2-3 KJV)

If you have read this devotional from the beginning, you already know I was raised a country girl. We had a huge garden which provided plenty of fresh vegetables all summer. My parents canned the excess so we could enjoy the fruits of their labor all winter. I wasn't a big fan of gardening back then. It was a chore—we all had to do our part. There was a lot of work to planting, weeding, harvesting, and preserving what we raised.

After I was married and had my daughter, I needed a way to earn some money and wanted to work from home. My husband suggested opening a small produce stand. He connected with some people and found places where I could buy whatever was in season at wholesale cost to sell it for a profit. As my business grew, I remembered the huge garden on the farm. Since much of my childhood was spent working in my family's garden, I assumed I could easily grow some of my own produce.

Unfortunately, I hadn't paid attention to some of the details involved in raising your own vegetables. My first venture of planting a big garden proved how little I knew about the process. It seems I knew more about the weeding, watering, and harvesting than how to get it all started.

A family friend, who had farmed for years, offered me lots of advice. He told me how deep in the ground to put the young plants and how far apart to place them. He explained what I needed to know about raising zucchini, cucumbers, squash, and beans from seed. His final suggestion was to buy some basic fertilizer. It would enrich the soil and improve my harvest.

I was confident I could do this and took everything he told me to heart. Only my thought was, *"if a little is good then a lot should really give me a big advantage."* After watering everything I'd planted, I poured a huge amount of fertilizer on all the tomato and pepper plants. The next morning, I walked out to look over my garden and got the surprise of my life. My plants were withered—bent over, limp, some lying flat on the ground. I literally cried. Quickly, I got in touch with the friend whose advice I'd followed —or so I thought. I yelled at him, "What happened? Everything is dying!"

"Calm down. What did you do?"

I explained how I'd planted everything. Then I told him about my brainstorm idea. "I was hoping to produce plenty of vegetables. So, I covered the tomatoes and peppers with lots and lots of fertilizer."

His response was loud and harsh, "No, no, no! You can't do that! I didn't realize I needed to mention that an overabundance of that stuff is way too strong for young plants. It'll kill them." He went into detail to make me understand. "They only needed a small circle of the nutrients sprinkled around them — at least two inches away from their tender roots. Sorry, you're probably going to have to pull out everything and toss it."

No way! I was not about to lose all my tomatoes and peppers. There just had to be something I could do to save them. I marched right out to the garden and desperately tried to dig away the excess fertilizer. Finally, with tears flowing and hands full of dirt, I was forced to admit he was right. None of my crop could be salvaged. This was an expensive mistake for me.

Thinking about how I frantically tried to push the excess of fertilizer away from my plants, the Lord put a thought in my heart. Too much of a good thing can be harmful. He brought to mind how overzealous I was when I first invited Him in to be the Lord of my life. There were times when all I did was nag, nag, and nag in my attempt to get my friends and family to accept Jesus as their Savior. But instead of wanting what I had, they were driven further away. At the time, I didn't understand what the problem was. God is good and what I was telling my loved ones was good. So, why were they turned off by what I was saying?

God made the answer to that question apparent by what happened with my plants. He was saying it *is* possible to give someone too much of even something as good as Bible verses. Just as I didn't help my plants with an excessive amount of fertilizer, I was not helping the spirits of the ones I chose to chase down with the gospel. Smothering them with scriptures was not helping. I was *killing* my friends and family — spiritually speaking.

I never stopped to consider where anyone was in their own personal journey with the Lord. Therefore, I was wasting my time when I attempted to shove God's Word down everyone's throats. Just because they didn't go to *my* church didn't mean they weren't already acquainted with Jesus. Stop "over-fertilizing" those we think we are called to "plant" in *our* church. Perhaps the Lord has picked out a different congregation for them to be a part of. God deals with each of us on an individual basis. Everyone doesn't need a long lecture on who Jesus is nor does everyone need to have the exact same kind of encounter with Him.

I am not saying it is wrong to share the joy of our salvation. But make sure the soil we are planting in has been made ready to receive the seeds. We can plant a few seeds as long as we do so in the right season. Then allow others do the watering so the seeds can sprout. Finally, realize it takes the Lord to bring anything to maturity.

It's all about timing. Allow God to open the doors of opportunity for us to speak about His goodness. He will, if the time is right. And remember to consider that some individuals have tender young roots. Breaking down the door to get into someone's heart is never the way to get inside.

Jesus himself gently pursues us as He waits for us to reach the turning point in our life. Let us do the same for others.

Being reminded of this whole episode in my garden made me think of how to approach someone when we share our faith. I thought it best to display our enthusiasm about our relationship with the Lord with more action and less words. Our best witness is actually just living out a changed life in front of those we care about. Be patient with others. Listen for the Lord's prompting to speak instead of chasing someone down to force the gospel on them.

Here are a few verses to remind us that God is the one who saves. We should be careful not to choke others with too much of the Good News. Let's be living examples! My challenge to us today is to see if we can point someone to Jesus without saying a word.

Let no man despise thy youth; but be thou an example of the believers, in word, in conversation, in charity, in spirit, in faith, in purity.
(I Tim. 4:12 KJV)

I have planted, Apollos watered; but God gave the increase. So then neither is he that planteth any thing, neither he that watereth; but God that giveth the increase.
(1 Cor. 3:6-7 KJV)

Lesson Fifteen
The Scent of Lilacs

"If the Son, therefore, shall make you free, ye shall be free indeed."
(John 8:36 KJV)

I didn't always walk the straight and narrow way. There was this other life I once lived. I refer to it as my life BC, Before Christ—before asking Jesus into my heart. Back then, I only knew *about* God. Lacking that personal relationship with Him caused me to make many bad decisions—ones that produced some undesirable habits. I depended on alcohol and cigarettes to cope with the stressful circumstances and situations I'd created. Not only did I become an alcoholic but I also developed all the symptoms of emphysema. I'd wake up in the morning with hangovers. With my head pounding, I'd cough until I actually vomited, then go outside and light up a cigarette. Why outdoors? Well, my husband didn't know I smoked; but that's another story.

After finally inviting Jesus to be the Lord of my life, I was determined to give complete control to Him. I was looking forward to turning my life around but couldn't seem to get a handle on my drinking and smoking. Ashamedly I put out my cigarettes before walking into church. I felt like someone stamped a big "guilty as charged" sign on my forehead every time I opened a beer. I was *convicted* but, unfortunately, I was also still *addicted*.

My husband, who had made no attempt to change his ways, asked me to come with him to meet friends for pizza and beer. We hadn't exactly been getting along since I'd started going to church, so I was excited about the date. I wasn't sure about going into the atmosphere of a bar. Ever since my spiritual encounter, I'd been doing my drinking at home. So, I came up with an excuse to give the Lord as to why I should go. I explained how I could let His light shine in a dark place.

This is how that idea played out. Once I started drinking, the alcohol took over. Before I knew it, I was drunk again. What an embarrassment I was to the Lord, slurring my words as I attempted to tell the old gang about my Jesus. As we left the establishment, my husband rudely reminded me he'd told me before we left, to leave Jesus at home. Our fight continued at home and it wasn't pretty. After that night, I definitely questioned this lifestyle I had once mistaken for being fun. There was no way I could continue with this type of behavior and call myself a servant of God.

When I first started following the Lord in a real way, I had gone to a recovery group to try to get help for my husband. I knew he was an alcoholic. As for me—I was just a social drinker; or so I thought. The person I spoke with had handed me a questionnaire to fill out about my own drinking patterns. When I left their office, I recall talking to myself— angry because they even considered giving it to me. I'd put it out of my sight that day. But now, I searched my house until I found it.

Question one: Do you sometimes drink more than you intended - check. Two: How often do you drink - daily got the check. Three: Does drinking negatively interfere with personal relationships – check. Four: Do you panic when you know you are out of alcohol – check. After answering everything on the survey, there it was. The truth was staring at me in black and white. I could no longer deny it—I was an alcoholic.

My cravings for beer and cigarettes had directed my actions and reactions for many years. Half-hearted attempts to cut back produced no lasting results. Completely stopping was definitely the only way out. I knew the Lord was asking me to let go. Later that night as I prayed, I made a commitment. "I promise, Lord, I'm going to quit." A friend told me she knew someone who could pray for me to be delivered from those nasty habits. I agreed to go with her to the person's house.

I'd been there before for a few Bible studies with my friend. Sometimes we'd seen someone being prayed for. They usually fell down to the floor when the leader laid hands on them. They called it "being slain in the spirit". I wasn't sure how I felt about all that even though I'd seen the same thing at my new church. I was a little nervous—not sure how this would all happen.

But it really wasn't scary at all. With my hands lifted towards heaven, I stood in front of the woman who was praying for everyone this particular evening. As tears streamed down my face, she asked God to set me free. My forehead was anointed with oil. With a loud voice, she commanded the spirits of alcohol and nicotine to come out. I felt an unseen force push me down. As I laid there on the floor — a peace swept over me. When my friend helped me up, the first thought in my head was, *"How could I have ever touched them?"* I wanted nothing to do with alcohol or cigarettes again — I was free. This was miraculous. My cravings were gone — they literally disappeared!

The most amazing part of what happened didn't become apparent until I got home. I walked around the corner of my house. The lilacs were in full bloom; their beautiful fragrance filled the air. I'd never smelled them without an allergic reaction. Something was different. I swallowed, touching my hand to my throat. How strange — my throat wasn't raw like it always was. I wasn't sneezing and my eyes weren't watering either. Lost in the moment, I stood on my porch taking one deep breath after another.

I teared up. How was this possible? Anyone who saw me might have thought I was crazy. I twirled around the porch as if I were dancing with the Lord. "Oh, my God! I can breathe down deep. I've been healed." I ran inside and rummaged through the junk drawer for a pair of scissors. I cut a huge bouquet of lilacs to grace my table — no reaction, no running nose. Savoring every whiff of their sweet scent, I continued my dance around the kitchen.

I could hardly believe my lungs were healed. I was never officially diagnosed, but am sure I suffered from the beginnings of emphysema. Before this deliverance, I coughed, gagged, and vomited every morning before I went outside to light up my cigarette. There was no more soreness — no more drainage. In the past, I'd quit smoking on my own for a day or two or sometimes even a few weeks. But my throat never improved. I still gagged on my own mucus daily. Today was different—my lungs were clear.

In the following weeks, I looked up towards heaven often. "God, how did you do this? How did you take my mind and turn my thinking around? How is it possible to now hate the things I loved?" The Lord reminded me of the scripture that began this story—the Son had set me free. No longer were those just words on a page. They had meaning. They were true. Freedom felt so good!

There is nothing like a real experience to make God's Word come alive. We serve a God who stands behind what he says and His Words have power. I've never forgotten how amazing this miracle was. Ever since that day I have asked the Lord to allow me to have a lilac bush wherever I live. And He has been faithful to answer my request. In fact, the little house I now live in helps me remember what a huge God I serve. He didn't give me just one lilac bush—He gave me four.

It has been over forty years since I experienced this great physical healing and I am still healed. I never craved a cigarette nor a drink after I was instantly delivered. And when Springtime comes, I thoroughly enjoy opening my windows and taking a deep breathe. Every scent of the lilacs reminds me that we serve a healing Jesus!

Bless the Lord, O my soul, and forget not all his benefits: Who forgiveth all thine iniquities; who healeth all thy diseases;
(Psalm 13:2-3 KJV)

And Jesus went about all the cities and villages, teaching in their synagogues, and preaching the gospel of the kingdom, and healing every sickness and every disease among the people.
(Matt. 9:35 KJV)

Excerpts of this story were taken from my novel published in November 2020 "From Curls to Cults – Breaking Free From Control". It is based on real life experiences — some of them my own. The book is available on Amazon.com.

Part Four

Lessons from Nature

16. Those Are My Peppers
17. Flow Like a River
18. Let God Plan Your Picnic
19. The Necessity of Change
20. Keep the Fire Burning
21. Harvesting Nuts
22. A Giver or a Taker

Lesson Sixteen

Those Are My Peppers

Ye have heard that it hath been said, Thou shalt love thy neighbour, and hate thine enemy. But I say unto you, Love your enemies, bless them that curse you, do good to them that hate you, and pray for them which despitefully use you, and persecute you; That ye may be the children of your Father which is in heaven: for he maketh his sun to rise on the evil and on the good, and sendeth rain on the just and on the unjust.
(Matt 5:43-45)

These scriptures are clear about what it means to love our enemies. They spell out the specifics; like returning blessings for curses or praying for those who despitefully use us. Despitefully is a strong word taken from Greek root words relating to retaliation against threats; it means to insult and slander or to falsely accuse. To pray for someone who did all that seems like a lot to ask of us. Of course, I didn't think I had to worry about that. I was sure I loved my enemies as the Word tells us to — but then came the test.

It was the first week of October in Ohio and time to harvest the last of my peppers before the frost hit. After a particularly hard day at work doing one of my part-time cleaning jobs, I went out to the garden and picked every last pepper—big, small, ripe, and even partially ripe. The oversized basket of peppers sitting on my back porch was piled high, above the rim. I smiled admiring the harvest. I was thinking, for my purposes, I surely had enough. It was one of my long-standing traditions to bless my family and friends with stuffed peppers at the end of the season. My plan was to cook lots of the peppers the next day. I had already bought everything I needed to stuff them—the ground meat, tomato juice and other ingredients.

This had not been a good year for the peppers. Because of the heat and rain patterns during the growing season many of them had a dry rot inside. The damage couldn't be detected until they were cut open. Still, I knew I would find plenty of the good ones. After getting out all the crock pots, I decided to wait until morning to sort through the peppers to find out which ones were clean inside. That decision is what led to the lesson God taught me about loving my enemies.

Allow me to give you some background information so you'll better understand where I'm coming from. I am sure there is one of these people in almost everyone's life—let's just call them The Moocher. They are the ones who never do anything for anyone unless there is something in it for themselves. I'm sure you've already pictured The Moocher in your own life—the one who has you tripping over all the strings attached every time they do a supposed favor for you. As far as you are concerned they are not a Christian. Why? Because that self-centered person has also been hateful and downright nasty to you over the years. In your eyes they are the enemy—you avoid them if at all possible.

The day I picked my peppers, The Moocher happened to stop by the farm and dropped off a couple dozen brown eggs we'd ordered from his neighbor. My sister was the one he'd spoken to. I wasn't even aware he'd been there—until the next morning. I had the huge basket of peppers on the table. Silently I whispered a prayer for most of them to be good as I began cutting them open. That's when my sister walked into the kitchen and said, "By the way, The Moocher saw your peppers on the porch last night. After I paid for the eggs, he said he sure would like some of those peppers since we have so many. And he pointed out how he had personally delivered our eggs."

I stared at her in unbelief, "Wait a minute, those are my peppers! I'm stuffing them for a least four different families, and his name is definitely not on my list!"

"I get it. He's never been anything but mean to you, but…"

"But what?" I snapped at her, "I won't do it! Besides, not all of these peppers are good. Lots of them have dry rot inside. I won't even know how many are okay to use until I get them all cleaned."

My sister, the calm, collected one answered so softly, "Really, it's okay. I was just going over there to see The Moocher with a question about my car. I'll stop at a road side stand and buy some peppers to give him. He'll never know the difference."

Busted—conviction was setting in. The Moocher had always been nasty to my sister too. Why was she willing to take him the peppers he asked for? I suddenly realized God was giving me a chance to be kind to someone who I thought really didn't deserve it. So, did I do a turnabout? Well, not exactly. Here's how it went down that day.

I grabbed a plastic bag and started picking out some peppers. At first I chose the worst-looking ones but soon realized that wasn't right either. So, I found ones that were about middle of the road in looks. But the way I put them in the bag was quite the sight. Throwing them in, I continued yelling at my sister who kept insisting I should just forget it — she would buy him some peppers. Then, I actually looked up to heaven and yelled at the Lord, "There, are you happy? I'm giving him the peppers! And I know I'm not getting any credit for this either, since I really don't want to do it."

I handed my sister the bag. "Here, give him the peppers. I know it's what I'm supposed to do!" With a frown on my face, I began the task of cutting and cleaning the peppers I had left. Each time I peered inside one I was sure it might be rotten. I figured I would deserve that. My attitude had been so rebellious when God was trying to show me how to extend love to someone I had labeled as unlovable. But I did find plenty of good peppers. I figured the Lord was teaching me the lesson and didn't want to upset those I had promised a meal to.

This isn't the end of my pepper story since I obviously failed the test. When I took a batch of stuffed peppers to my Pastor's wife and told her this story, she had some advice for me. She looked at me and said, "You know what you have to do, don't you?"

"And what might that be?" I asked.

She looked so serious when she told me her recommendation. "Next year, when you pick your peppers, you need to fix The Moocher a batch of stuffed peppers and send them to him." I sighed, knowing she was telling me the truth. I hate tests and didn't want to keep retaking the same one. Besides, who knows what the Lord would ask of me next time if I still didn't learn my lesson.

One year later, I took her advice and made that extra batch of stuffed peppers for The Moocher. I decided to put the three crock pots of peppers on before I went to bed. I set them on low so they would be done in the morning. Then I could deliver them to everyone.

When I came down to the kitchen very early in the morning I thought I smelled something burning. Sure enough, my small crock pot cooked differently than my newer large ones and some of the peppers had stuck to the bottom and sides and burned. I quickly took them out of the tomato juice broth and tried to salvage them. I tried to convince myself that maybe they tasted just a little burnt and I could give those to The Moocher.

Immediately, I heard a voice in my head ask if they would be good enough for my Pastor and his wife. I knew the answer to that and I wasn't about to take this test over. After delivering the other peppers I'd promised, I stopped at the store and purchased several very nice peppers, more meat, and other ingredients. Yes, I came home and made a great bunch of peppers for The Moocher and my sister delivered them. Finally, I passed the test—minus a few points for thinking I could give him the burnt ones.

The Lord reminded me that being kind to someone who hurt me did not mean I condoned their actions. He just wanted to make sure I wasn't holding a grudge. My mindset needed to change. It is okay to hate wrongdoing, evil, and sin but I had to learn to pray for the sinner. Jesus said he didn't wish that any would perish.

When this all started, my attitude made me become The Moocher. I decided I wasn't going to give freely anything to someone who would never give me anything in return. Jesus taught the opposite of what I was doing.

And I would like to add a thought. What the Lord asks each of us to do with The Moocher in our lives can be different. God never expects us to become a doormat who allows abuse to go on forever. This was something He was requiring of me in a particular season in my life. Be still and listen to what He may be asking you to do. He may just let you keep your peppers simply because you already have a good attitude! I will leave you with a few scriptures to think about.

And if ye lend to them of whom ye hope to receive, what thank have ye? for sinners also lend to sinners, to receive as much again. But love ye your enemies, and do good, and lend, hoping for nothing again; and your reward shall be great, and ye shall be the children of the Highest: for he is kind unto the unthankful and to the evil.
(Luke 6:34-35 KJV)

Dearly beloved, avenge not yourselves, but rather give place unto wrath: for it is written, Vengeance is mine; I will repay, saith the Lord. Therefore if thine enemy hunger, feed him; if he thirst, give

him drink: for in so doing thou shalt heap coals of fire on his head. Be not overcome of evil, but overcome evil with good.
(Romans 12:19-21 KJV)

Lesson Seventeen

Flow Like a River

He that believeth on me, as the scripture hath said, out of his belly shall flow rivers of living water.
(John 7:38 KJV)

"Enough is enough! I thought the rainy season was supposed to be in the spring." That's what my cries to the Lord sounded like for several weeks. It was past mid-July and my tomato, pepper, cucumber, and zucchini plants were literally drowning. My garden sat in a low area so the nonstop rain had completely immersed the bottom half of my once hardy plants. They were drooping—wilted and yellow. Any tiny new vegetables were rotting on the branches.

Weeks before the downpours started, I had already picked some great looking tomatoes—big and solid. And the zucchini and cucumber plants had been producing since late in June. So, the sight of my sorry-looking garden was frustrating to say the least. It took a lot of hard work to get it to where it was before the rains came. I wasn't ready to settle for a small harvest. I decided I could fix this.

After carefully looking over the lay of the land I figured out where I needed to start digging. It was quite the process to get the water to flow away from the plants. I had to dig really deep ditches in some of the areas to correct the drainage problem. Eventually it happened—the puddles became rivers. It made me smile to see the water rushing away. Even when we got additional very heavy rainfall, the plants only received the moisture they needed. As long as I kept the ditches clear, the water moved.

What happened then amazed me. The tomato and pepper plants grew new branches. The primary vines must have had deep roots which were still strong. New blossoms appeared! And I was able to harvest more vegetables later that year. After I pruned the rotted vegetables off the cucumber and zucchini plants, they also bore more fruit.

When I first began trying to save my plants, God reminded me we are called to have rivers of living water flowing out of our belly. When Jesus referred to the belly in the verses in the book of John, He didn't mean our abdomen. The Greek word used for belly in this scripture means the matrix—the center where something develops. Figuratively, it's the womb or the heart. Whenever someone is in our womb or in our heart, they are precious. If we are pregnant, the special one is the baby we are carrying. If we're in love, our thoughts are fixed on the one with whom we're forming a relationship.

Sometimes in our human mind it is hard to comprehend— God lives in us. What a privilege! Once we grasp that He dwells in our hearts, we will gladly keep the Lord as our central focus. Bragging about Him and talking about His goodness will be a natural thing. What is in our hearts almost always manifests by what we speak. All we have to do is open our mouths. Let the greatness of who He is and what He has done for us pour out. That is the message of the scripture I began this story with. The "rivers of living water" are our words proclaiming the wonders of Jesus to the world.

After I salvaged my garden, I thought back on how pitiful it looked before it was drained. It made me wonder about the way we act sometimes. Maybe we don't always allow the Spirit of God to flow back out to bless those around us. If we sit in church and just soak in the spirit for ourselves, we might become water-logged. These thoughts certainly made me take a deeper look inside. It's great to get filled with living water, which is the Spirit of God. But if we hold it all in, we might become bloated. Before long we'll look just like my drowning plants. Spiritually speaking we, the branches, will become limp and weak—finally withering. We'll produce no fruit; or at best rotten fruit.

Anything we receive from the Lord is always meant to be shared with others. I don't want to be stingy or lazy and keep the good news to myself. Then I'd be like a stagnant pond that gives nothing back to the environment around it. It gathers moss, breeds mosquitoes, and it stinks. I don't know about you, but I don't want to be a stinky Christian.

On the other hand, rivers are fresh and clean—able to provide water for those who are thirsty. Living things can survive in running waters. The Lord was letting me know He expects us to keep the message moving. He wants us to let what we take in flow back out to the thirsty souls around us.

My pathetic fruitless plants also made me think about the whole fruit bearing process. I found a scripture about this in John 15:2 *Every branch in me that beareth not fruit he taketh away: and every branch that beareth fruit, he purgeth it, that it may bring forth more fruit.*

At first, it sounded like it was the end of the road for a branch that wasn't producing. It says they would be taken away. Sometimes we have to dig a little deeper to find out what Jesus was saying. Going back to Greek, the original language the words were written in, is where I found the answer. I discovered that word *airo* was translated "taketh away" in these verses. However, that same word in eight other places in the New Testament is translated as lifted, lifted up, taken up, or picked up. Therefore, a more accurate translation of John 15:2 might read, *every branch in me that beareth not fruit he lifts up.*

I absolutely think this is how this scripture should read. Why? Because I looked into how true vinedressers operate. They don't just discard an unfruitful branch. As long as it's connected to the vine, caregivers do everything possible to help it. Those branches are handled gently as they are *lifted up* to rest on trellises. They are repositioned to give them more sun; the soil around them is checked for nourishment.

This was so encouraging! After analyzing the verse in John, I realized it is much more consistent with Jesus' character for Him to lift us up and guide us to where we need to be. Rest assured, we don't need to worry about being cut off and thrown away if we don't seem to possess all the spiritual fruits.

The Lord demonstrated several truths to me through the ordeal of my drowning garden. He wanted me to make sure I didn't become a lazy and unproductive Christian. He desires all of us to open our mouths and let the gospel flow out of our innermost beings. I pray you are sharing the Lord with those around you. But if not, please remember He is always willing to pick us up; especially if we've fallen short because we've gotten too full and kept it all to ourselves. Think on His great mercy as you read these scriptures. Let's keep the message of His love flowing!

He hath not dealt with us after our sins; nor rewarded us according to our iniquities. For as the heaven is high above the earth, so great is his mercy toward them that fear him. As far as the east is from the west, so far hath he removed our transgressions from us.
(Ps. 103:10-12 KJV)

Who is a God like unto thee, that pardoneth iniquity, and passeth by the transgression of the remnant of his heritage? he retaineth not his anger for ever, because he delighteth in mercy. He will turn again, he will have compassion upon us; he will subdue our iniquities; and thou wilt cast all their sins into the depths of the sea.
(Micah 7:18-19 KJV)

Scriptures from John about the vine can be found printed in the back of this book.

Lesson Eighteen

Let God Plan Your Picnic

Trust in the Lord with all thine heart; and lean not unto thine own understanding. In all thy ways acknowledge him, and he shall direct thy paths.
(Prov. 3:5-6 KJV)

The Fourth of July picnic was going to be at my house this year. It was sort of a combination party to celebrate the holiday and to say good-bye to the farmhouse I was raised in. This would be my last summer there. After my parents passed, my sister and I bought the house and lived there for several years. Since our lives were going in different directions, we decided to go our separate ways. The house was on the market so it would only be a matter of time–this was a final family get together and I wanted it to be perfect.

I am a planner and had the menu and lists of everything that needed to be done to make it a party to remember. Incidentally, my sister who shared the home with me is more of a last-minute person. She had to work the day before so I assigned her a few little things to be responsible for. I asked her to do the grilling and make her fabulous strawberry pies the morning of the fourth.

This year we had a really rainy summer towards the end of June. But it had finally stopped the first days of July and dried most of the puddles that had formed in our uneven yard. Now, I had to catch up on mowing our huge country yard. Everyone who knows me is well aware of how overly-particular I am about how the lawn looks. I never let anyone do it for me because I don't want all those ugly piles of dead grass setting on it. It has to be perfect—trimmed and raked.

It was a warm day when I stepped outside to check out the weather so I could begin mowing on the third of July. This was a big job and it would take several hours. Even though it looked cloudy, I decided to go to a store and get the buns before starting the lawn. The planner in me insisted that the buns needed to be fresh. They couldn't be bought until today. This morning of the third my human logic told me I had better get the buns *now* because sometimes stores run out of them on summer holidays. I guess I didn't think God was capable of saving me several packs of buns.

When I got home, I immediately jumped on the mower. After two swipes around the big side lot, it started raining. And it wasn't just a little—it was torrential. As I rushed the mower to the garage I was weeping. I looked up and yelled at God, "You could have stayed the rain!" Thinking back on my rant, I am grateful we serve a merciful God who understands our frustrations.

After changing my dripping wet clothes, I went to the other store in the opposite direction of the one I'd gone to in the morning. This time I went to buy the ground beef. Yes, the meat was another last-minute purchase since it had to be fresh—not frozen.

Surprisingly, the downpour ended just as quickly as it began. Nevertheless, the yard was wet. But since it had come down so hard most of the rain had run off and not soaked in. By the time I got home, a strong wind had come up—strong enough to dry the grass to the point where it could be cut. My sister's granddaughter, who came from out-of-town, jumped on our spare riding mower. We finished the yard in half the time it would have taken me. And she made sure it was all raked.

In the flesh I was weak. I'd made an angry outburst—accusing God of mismanaging His world by letting it rain. After it all worked out, I could see how foolish it was for me to be anxious over the lawn. But apparently, God didn't think I'd learned how to trust Him yet. He had another lesson prepared to prove to me how He can handle any situation.

I woke up excited about the party–today was the Fourth of July. Immediately, I began checking my lists of exactly what time to prepare each dish so it would all be ready for the picnic scheduled for 2:00 in the afternoon. I had already explained to my sister we had everything we needed for food. I was baking chicken inside. She just needed to get those pies done and be ready to light our small gas grill at 1:15. If she started the burgers and hotdogs at 1:30, I could keep them all warm in the oven.

Well, my last-minute sister decided to make her famous potato salad the morning of the fourth. The problem is, her salad takes a long time to prepare—time not figured in on *my* lists. Plus, it was going to make a big mess in our small kitchen. I said we didn't need it but she's never listened to me before and wasn't going to let it be a first today. She began boiling the potatoes and eggs. It was 1:30 before my sister went out to light grill. At 1:40 she walks back inside and announces, "That which I feared has come upon me, our grill is out of gas."

My reaction was once again shouting. Only it was directed at her. "No! This can't be happening! The party is due to begin at 2:00. I'll have to "George Foreman" the burgers and dogs! Who wants food grilled inside on the fourth?"

My sister responded in the way she usually does. No panic—just trust. "The neighbor will help me get the tank off. I'll take it to the Convenient Store and exchange it for a full one." She did just that—got home and grilled burgers and hot dogs.

It was a great picnic. And, guess what? Everyone didn't arrive exactly at 2:00. The ones who did didn't say, "Where's the food? We want to eat right now!" Anxiety caused me to be upset over things that really didn't matter. God has a different timeline. He wasn't being mean—not caring about messing up my plans. He merely wanted me to relax and believe He is capable! On a side note, the potato salad *was* the favorite dish at the picnic.

No one knew we were "off" schedule. Resting in the Lord means going with the flow when plans change. It's never about us. It's not wrong to make lists and have goals. But we also need to be prepared for real life—nothing ever goes exactly as we want it to! I know God changed my agenda to see who I was depending on. Even though I failed that test I won't give up on myself. You shouldn't give up on yourself either.

We all have room for improvement. From my personal experiences, I know the Lord grades on a big curve. My prayer is for all of us to learn how to place everything in His hands. He has every detail of our lives under control. Someday I hope we all stop having to take our tests over. Lean on Him! His plans leave nothing to chance!

Commit thy way unto the Lord; trust also in him; and he shall bring it to pass.
(Psalm 37:5 KJV)

Be careful for nothing; but in every thing by prayer and supplication with thanksgiving let your requests be made known unto God. And the peace of God, which passeth all understanding, shall keep your hearts and minds through Christ Jesus.
(Phil. 4:6-7 KJV)

Lesson Nineteen

The Necessity of Change

To everything there is a season, and a time to every purpose under the heaven:
(Ecc. 3:1 KJV)

I was outside preparing everything for the changes that were about to happen as we transitioned from fall into winter. There was a lot to do getting ready to protect a number of things from the shift in the weather patterns. My many wood and metal plant stands and yard decorations had to be put in the shed. Other larger items just needed to be covered so they wouldn't be damaged by the snow that would soon blanket the ground. Plastic was put over the windows of the shed as an extra layer of protection against winter storms. A special shelter was made for our cat who spent his whole life outdoors—extra straw was added to the places in the old garage where he would snuggle up on very cold winter nights. Seasons bring change. Change—it's not something we always look forward to.

Nevertheless, what occurs in nature is established. Winter, spring, summer, and fall combine and overlap each other to make a complete year. It will always happen until the end of time. Just as in the natural world, so it is in the spiritual. This journey we are on is one season overlapping another until it makes a complete life. We all mature and grow old as we go through our individual ever-changing circumstances.

Each natural season is usually identified in a certain way. Spring is a time of planting, rebirth, new beginnings, and renewal. Summer is a time of looking ahead, relaxation, and beauty. Fall is the time of harvest, hard work, and enjoying the fruits of our labor. Winter is a time of waiting, dreariness, or even darkness. In the spirit we experience similar types of seasons that mimic the natural ones. God's Word declares every season is unique. It is marked by particular events, challenges, necessities, purposes, and lessons.

Seasons cannot stand alone in the natural or spiritual — they're nourished by the preceding seasons. Each depends on the other for preparation and for fulfillment of purpose. To have a complete life we cannot skip going through the hard seasons. Nor can we choose to always remain in the ones we like best. All are needed because growth is impossible without experiencing changes.

We are creatures of comfort and attempt to avoid what is unpleasant. We become accustomed to enjoying life when all is smooth sailing. So, we throw out our anchor. But regardless of which seasons we prefer; life never allows us to stay in the ones that are sunshine and roses forever. Ready or not, the changeovers to what we don't like will come!

Discovering God on the Farm

Life is about choices. So, we decide whether to sit and pout when things go awry or to keep moving forward. It's the only way to learn the lessons we are being taught. We are being built-up in ways we sometimes won't realize until we look back. As we navigate through the challenges of all four seasons, transformations are happening. Our stamina is strengthened. Our character is shaped. Each particular season prepares us for whatever we may have to face in all of our tomorrows — especially the ones that are undesirable.

We all experience the seasons in different ways and the seasons themselves have variations such as harsh winters or extremely hot summers. But there is one thing they all have in common. Every season requires us to adjust to its conditions. So let's take a closer look at what happens in nature. If God provides ways for the plants and animals to adapt, He certainly has plans to help us survive the ever-changing seasons of life.

In the animal kingdom, when what is normal is interrupted, one means of coping is called dormancy. It's a period in a life cycle when growth, development, and, in animals, physical activity is temporarily stopped according to environmental conditions. Many times, it can be predicted. There are signs that warn of the changes therefore preparations can be made.

There is also consequential dormancy. It occurs when unexpected adverse conditions arise — like droughts. Some animals seem to have warning systems built in to let them know when winters will be harsher or last longer. Those are the ones who take more time to prepare for the unusual droughts or extra-long and cold seasons. But, in nature, sudden changes in conditions lead to higher mortality rates because not all animals plan ahead.

So, it is with us. Sometimes we are able to prepare for the dormant phases of life. Nevertheless, we all have those times when we are faced with the unexpected. Overwhelming trials, situations, or circumstances happen. Incurable diseases attack our bodies, loved ones die prematurely, financial crises arise, and families fall apart. Such occurrences can cause us to come to a standstill in our spiritual growth. Sometimes, they even cause us to question our faith.

Although we can't predict when detrimental things will take place, we have the Lord as our warning system. Developing and maintaining a close relationship with Him is how we prepare ahead of time. Trust God to be our strength when faced with adverse situations. Remain focused on the big picture—on the eternal. With the Lord at the center of our lives, adverse circumstances don't need to be fatal.

Plant species also go through dormancy. They have a biological clock that tells them when to slow activity and to prepare soft tissues for a period of freezing temperatures or water shortage. The Spirit of the Lord is our biological clock—leading us, guiding us, telling us there may be trouble around the bend. Believe that God is able to provide a survival strategy no matter how big our problems look. Then we won't just *dry up and die* when a dire situation hits us in the face. He is our peace in the middle of our storms.

Hibernation is another part of the dormant process. Many mammals use this to escape the cold weather and food shortages over the winter. Before they can retreat and rest there is much groundwork to be done. An animal prepares by building up a thick layer of body fat during late summer and fall. This will provide energy during their periods of isolation.

During our summers and autumns, we should store up God's Word so we can speak it over our troubles. It will sustain us during our long dark winter seasons. It will help us hold onto an inner calm in the midst of unexpected famines. Those times when we have to go into hibernation, we can live off the layers of His Word we have hidden in our hearts. Never stop gathering and preparing our spirits for whatever our future may hold.

Another interesting type of dormancy is called diapause. It is slowing down metabolism to delay the birthing of offspring because they would die if they're born at the wrong time — a time when the environment's conditions are not favorable. Maybe we should consider diapause as part of our strategic planning. Sometimes as we attempt to "birth" new ministries, we get over-anxious about launching everything. Waiting on God's timing isn't always easy but it may be necessary for survival. Things birthed outside of the right season can die.

The same is also true if we are attempting to bring an individual to experience a new spiritual birth. Always listen for the prompting of the Lord as we witness to those whom we think *need* to turn over a new leaf. Be patient — perhaps it isn't their time yet.

Nature is fascinating. It demonstrates how the Lord has ordained specific times for plants, insects, and animals to go through the process of change. This ensures they live long productive lives. How much more will He guide us through our seasons of life? My prayer for today is this. Learn to enjoy our summers. Be willing to work hard during the harvest time. Prepare for the winters. Trust God — spring is coming!

While the earth remaineth, seedtime and harvest, and cold and heat, and summer and winter, and day and night shall not cease.
(Gen. 8:22 KJV)

These things I have spoken unto you, that in me ye might have peace. In the world ye shall have tribulation: but be of good cheer; I have overcome the world.
(John 16:33 KJV)

Lesson Twenty

Keep the Fire Burning

Let your loins be girded about, and your lights burning;
(Luke 12:35 KJV)

The day of my salvation—what a glorious day that was. I vividly remember leaving the church feeling so clean and so loved. Literally, I was wondering if anyone could see me glowing. The dark heavy veil of sin and guilt had been lifted off. Suddenly, I was head over heels in love with Jesus—and I knew He loved me in the same way.

It was just like when young couples fall for each other. They usually have that special glow about them. It's obvious to all who cross paths with them—they're in love. Visualize a proud groom waiting for his bride to walk down the aisle and put her hand in his at the altar. We've all seen the look on his face—that radiance. That's exactly how it is the day we first surrender and make the commitment to wholeheartedly follow Jesus. I'm sure many of us remember the exact place, date, and time it happened. But mostly we remember the feeling—our hearts being ablaze with love for the Lord.

Jesus wants us to always feel that way. After all, it's His light shining through us that expels the darkness in the world. Unfortunately, life happens. What goes on in the spirit world is exactly like what takes place in the natural. As time goes on, couples settle into routines—they get comfortable with their circumstances. Before they realize it, they start taking each other for granted. The flame of the romance begins to flicker and fade. And so it is with our spirits. We sometimes forget the passion we had when we first felt that overwhelming love of Jesus. We lose our glow—our light grows dim. In both marriages and our relationship with the Lord it takes work to keep the love-light bright.

The scripture I began this lesson with talks about just that—keeping our lights burning. Jesus was giving instructions concerning what we need to do while watching for his return to claim His bride. One evening, when I was trying to start a real campfire, the Lord made it clear to me as to why the flame needs to be kept alive.

There is safety around a brightly burning campfire. Many times, the dancing flames keep wild animals away. Annoying bugs can't get near the heat of the fire either. How much more does this same concept apply in the spirit? When our fire is blazing, it helps to keep the devil away. He's the one prowling about like a roaring lion seeking anyone he may devour. When our passion for the Lord is still raging in our heart, we will be able to deter any demons. They're the distracting pests, who have plenty of annoying plans to get us off course. They can't stand the heat and won't be able to get close enough to hurt us.

As I alluded to, I was *attempting* to get a fire going in my backyard. My great-niece was over and we thought we would roast some marshmallows. The only problem was that it had rained really hard that day. Actually, it had been pouring for several days. Our wood pile was soaked. But I wasn't about to miss a chance to have a s'more. I scrounged through every stack of wood. Looking underneath, I found a little kindling that wasn't completely saturated and what seemed to be dryer logs—or so I thought. Then I rolled up huge amounts of newspapers and lit the match. The papers immediately burst into flames. Unfortunately, they didn't burn quite long enough to start the kindling. To no avail I kept adding paper. As a last resort my sister found some lighter fluid and began squirting it on the wood that had one tiny ember. She kept it up and kept it up. A flame would appear for a moment—but we still weren't able to ignite the wet wood. Sad to say, we gave up.

So what was wrong here? Basically, these logs were full of the wrong thing. It was something on the inside of the logs that made them not able to burn. Maybe, that's what happens when our light goes out. We sometimes let our spirit soak up the wrong things. Whatever we've allowed to come through our eye gates or ear gates will find its way into our hearts and spirits. When we become careless and let inappropriate things in, our flesh ends up ruling our actions. We become waterlogged—our lights no longer shine.

Or perhaps we've listened to a watered-down gospel for so long that we can't get our flame to ignite. We may still look like a Christian on the outside but what we've stored up inside is causing our flame to grow dim. We can't fool God. He sees through whatever masks we've put on and knows what's in our innermost being. I am so grateful He doesn't give up on us like we gave up on our campfire. What a wonderful Savior! He never gets tired of trying to fan our dying embers as He draws us back to Him.

We can't afford to get apathetic about our relationship with the Lord. People are looking for something to brighten their days—looking for a better tomorrow. When our love light gets dim, the good news of the gospel no longer invades those dark, hopeless places in the world.

What could have fixed my water-logged wood? It needed the "sun" to penetrate it. Likewise, we need to let the "Son" penetrate every fiber of our being. It's time to take our Bibles out of the corner, crack them open, and fill ourselves with God's words. When His words drench our inner most being, we'll begin to shine from the inside out.

In the present times we are living in, Jesus is calling us, His church, to ignite any tiny sparks within until they become a bright raging fire. Let's find the joy of our first love once again. Be the beacon of His light! My prayer is that we will be so ablaze for Jesus that the world can't help but see Him!

Restore unto me the joy of thy salvation; and uphold me with thy free spirit. Then will I teach transgressors thy ways; and sinners shall be converted unto thee.
(Psalm 51:12-13 KJV)

Ye are the light of the world. A city that is set on an hill cannot be hid. Neither do men light a candle, and put it under a bushel, but on a candlestick; and it giveth light unto all that are in the house. Let your light so shine before men, that they may see your good works, and glorify your Father which is in heaven.
(Matt. 5:14-16 KJV)

Lesson Twenty-One

Harvesting Nuts

Do you not say, 'There are still four months and then comes the harvest'? Behold, I say to you, lift up your eyes and look at the fields, for they are already white for harvest!
(John 4:35-36 KJV)

Harvest time is a wonderful time but it represents a lot of hard work. There are a variety of ways to gather the fruits of your labor depending on what it is. Timing is everything since the state of maturity is different for each individual fruit or vegetable. Some need to be gathered before a frost as they cannot withstand the cold — others are considered better after a frost. A farmer has to be knowledgeable about the right time to pick whatever he has grown. He may have grains. Those crops involve reaping, threshing, winnowing, and storing — it requires an understanding of the process.

Jesus taught in the scriptures about the harvest. It is interesting to see how He painted those pictures of nature to teach us spiritual concepts. The Lord brought some such analogies to my mind the year I attempted to harvest our walnuts.

My parents had always done all the work of gathering the nut crop. All of us children only saw the finished product. We were all blessed with containers full of delicious shelled walnuts—ready to eat or put in our favorite recipes. When my parents were no longer with us, one of my sisters and I continued living in the farmhouse for several years. It was fall and I was desperately trying to remember whatever I could about harvesting the nuts. It soon became apparent that I'd paid little attention to the process.

About the only thing I'd recalled was seeing bags of nuts hanging in the basement to dry. So, I found a bunch of the old mesh bags and filled them with the nuts. I felt so proud when I got them all secured—tied to the clothes lines down there. After a while it seemed like I smelled a musty odor coming from the bags. I took some nuts out to check them. It was a disaster! All of the nuts were molded—rotted inside. It was then I realized the outer hull had to be removed before putting them in the bags.

The Lord reminded me of the scriptures about harvesting souls for His kingdom. Many of the people who gather into our churches have that hull—a hard wall that covers what is inside. For some it's barricades they have built around their core for protection from the pain of past hurts. For others it's years of making the wrong choices and living sinful lives. Regardless of what someone is hiding behind, before the good inside can surface, the thick outer layer needs to be removed.

In nature the hull is the part of the walnut that contains a stain. It is messy and dirty to remove it. Sometimes when wayward souls find their way into our churches, we keep our distance from them. We don't want to get too involved with helping to remove the layers to get to what is inside — it could be messy. Breaking the cycles of hurtful experiences or of wayward lifestyles isn't easy. The process can be a tedious job. But it will be worth the effort if we take the time to help others remove those hard layers.

Let us never forget that there are underlying reasons for every person's behavior. Those who come seeking the Lord, stained by unpleasant memories or by sins, may not be totally at fault for their situations. May we always act and react with patience and compassion. That's what Jesus did!

Jesus appealed to His followers about being willing to do the work — emphasizing how the harvest was great but the laborers were few. This made me think about that first year of attempting to harvest the nut crop. It would have been so much better to have *learned* what my parents did instead of just reaping the proceeds of their hard work all those years ago. I so wished I had paid attention and asked to help along the way. Then I would've known exactly how to gather and store the nuts. As the old saying goes, "A little hard work never killed anyone."

The next year my harvesting of the walnuts went much better. I removed that outer hull and hung the nuts in bags to dry. Success, but after that came the task of cracking the nuts open to get to the meat. This process should be done in a specific way as to not crush the insides. It takes skill to crack the shell and be able to produce a whole walnut — unbroken and ready for nourishing our bodies.

It also takes a great skill to be able to break the last bits of hard layers off someone's inner being. And of course, we want to keep a person's soul together—unbroken. When we do it correctly, that person will eventually be able to pass it on—provide spiritual nourishment for others.

Some walnuts have extra-hard shells. I discovered they are easier to crack if they're soaked in water. Water generally is symbolic of the spirit of the Lord. We might consider giving any new individuals who come into God's family time to soak in the spirit. It could be less complicated if we allowed His spirit to soften hearts so they'll be able to open up to what the Lord has for them. When He prepares a heart, it is not likely to be broken during the healing process.

Let us all be willing to work hard as we go about doing the work of the final gathering of the lost into God's kingdom. If we look at the world today I am sure we can agree—there is a great harvest of souls about to happen. There is plenty of work to be done. But, let's prepare to spread the gospel in a kinder, less judgmental way. If we do things God's way, we can bring countless individuals to the knowledge of the Lord. Then the harvest will be plenteous!

Therefore, said he unto them, The harvest truly is great, but the labourers are few: pray ye therefore the Lord of the harvest, that he would send forth labourers into his harvest.
(Luke 10:2 KJV)

So that servant came, and shewed his lord these things. Then the master of the house being angry said to his servant, Go out quickly

into the streets and lanes of the city, and bring in hither the poor, and the maimed, and the halt, and the blind. And the servant said, Lord, it is done as thou hast commanded, and yet there is room. And the lord said unto the servant, Go out into the highways and hedges, and compel them to come in, that my house may be filled.
(Luke 14:21-23 KJV)

Lesson Twenty-Two

A Giver or a Taker

Jesus answered them and said, Verily, verily, I say unto you, Ye seek me, not because ye saw the miracles, but because ye did eat of the loaves, and were filled.
(John 6:26 KJV)

I never minded cutting the grass in my huge country yard. In fact, I rather enjoyed it because I love being outdoors. As I was moving along on the riding mower, I went in between trees in the back yard making several passes around the stumps left from some nut trees. Early in the spring a friend cut them down—one had not produced any fruit for years and the other had been killed by a harsh winter. They were both quite unsightly and needed to be removed. However, my friend had left a two-foot-high piece of the trunk standing from each tree.

The one tree was actually still alive at the roots when it was cut down. Thus, the trunk left in the ground had lots of very thin leafy branches growing out of it. In fact, you couldn't even see it. It looked like a weird bush not a stump—

unrecognizable, completely covered. Then, as I made a few more swipes, I noticed the other productive trees in the yard also had lots of those stray branches growing out of their trunks. We had always referred to these extensions as suckers because they suck life from the tree but produce no fruit. They certainly detract from the beauty of a tree.

As I continued to mow, the Lord brought some thoughts to my mind. He began comparing those suckers to our relationships with Him. He is the vine, the trunk if you will. As the scripture says we are the branches, expected to bear fruit. I began wondering about my relationship with the Lord. Was I a real branch, a true extension of the trunk, ready to display some fruit in my life or was I just a sucker?

A sucker hangs on and takes all the nourishment out of the trunk. It doesn't in any way give anything back. I didn't want to be attached to Jesus just for what he could do for me. Then I stopped myself from walking down the path of self-condemnation. It's natural to want the Lord to be our provider. It only becomes a problem when it is the *only* reason for clinging to Him.

As I finished cutting the grass, I continued thinking about what being a productive bearer of fruit looks like. It took me back to when I was in love. All I thought about then was what I could do for my special someone. Since the most important fruit is love, it has to start there. It's not truly love when only one party in a twosome is trying to make the other feel special. To bond or connect with anyone requires give and take from both sides. It's what enables the love to grow into a worthwhile relationship.

Jesus promised the abundant life but being the recipient of His promises is a two-way street. All things will be *given* to us but there are "qualifying" clauses connected to this promise. Sometimes we ignore those parts of a scripture—the ones that let us know what is expected of us.

Our connection to the Lord becomes lopsided when we only look at what's in it for us. If all of our prayers consist of long lists of give me, give me, give me, we need to do some serious soul searching. If we're only hanging onto the Lord for the tangible things—sucking the life out of Him, we're distracting from His beauty.

When acquiring possessions becomes our goal, we miss what is truly important in this life. And unfortunately, when we as Christians focus on the wrong things, we make Jesus look ugly to the world—just like all those suckers make the trees look ugly.

I was reminded of Job, who was able to praise the Lord even after losing everything. He had the right attitude when he said, *"Naked came I out of my mother's womb, and naked shall I return thither: the Lord gave, and the Lord hath taken away; blessed be the name of the Lord." (Job 1:21 KJV)* Job was put to the test. He proved he wasn't serving God just for what He could give him.

If we have been fortunate enough to have walked in nothing but blessings, we should always be mindful of our innermost thoughts. Don't allow greediness to come creeping in. It is easy to sometimes start expecting more from where *that* came from. Instead, we should think about sharing some of the abundance the Lord has allowed us to have. When we do, His provisions will bring Him glory by pointing others to the source of all good things.

When we walk in favor, it is also sometimes easy to put our Bible on the shelf. Be careful not to forget about the Lord. When we momentarily forget the one who showered us with His goodness, we might be the one responsible for stopping the flow of God's generosity. Even though we are king's kids, we shouldn't expect everything to be handed to us on a silver platter. Instead, we should use our privileged position to improve the world around us.

I encourage us all to seek Jesus for the right reasons. Be a true reflection of Him to the world. Make the Lord easy to recognize instead of covering Him up with self-centered requests. Look for more opportunities to be open-handed. The Lord will direct our path to those who have real needs. Self-examine—I did the day I was mowing. I never want to be a worthless taker who blocks the true beauty of Jesus. Be a giver—not a taker!

I have shewed you all things, how that so labouring ye ought to support the weak, and to remember the words of the Lord Jesus, how he said, It is more blessed to give than to receive.
(Acts 20:35 KJV)

Jesus said unto him, If thou wilt be perfect, go and sell that thou hast, and give to the poor, and thou shalt have treasure in heaven: and come and follow me.
(Matt. 19:21 KJV)

Part Five

He is Still Speaking

23. Broken Pottery

24. Hidden Sin

25. My Ugly Oak Tree

26. Praise Him in the Storm

Lesson Twenty-Three

Broken Pottery

Then I went down to the potter's house, and, behold, he wrought a work on the wheels. And the vessel that he made of clay was marred in the hand of the potter: so he made it again another vessel, as seemed good to the potter to make it.
(Jer. 18:3-4)

The pandemic of 2020 — who would've ever imagined we'd find ourselves in quarantine? My state shut down, literally. All non-essential workers were on stay-at-home orders. Suddenly, I couldn't go into the private houses I cleaned to supplement my income on a part-time basis. There I was, home alone; isolated from loved ones. So began my lists — lists of things that I'd always wanted to do but never found the time. Yes, I am one of those people who love crossing things off of my list. There is something so satisfying about making that check mark — done!

After spending much of the first month deep-cleaning my house, I got to the fun part. These were the many projects I'd put aside for years thinking I didn't have time to do them.

Now, I had nothing but time. The weather was warming so my thoughts turned to what I might do outdoors.

As I stared out my kitchen window, I saw the old pottery Dutch Boy beneath the lilac bush. Ever since I'd moved into my house, he'd been standing there. His head had been glued back on by the previous owner. You could barely see what was left of the faded yellow polka dots on his pants. He was quite unsightly, mostly a gray mess. Many a day I had wanted to kick him to the curb but he is heavy — thus he remained. A few years back I'd painted his partner, the little Dutch Girl. She looked adorable amid some flowers and bushes in my backyard. Today, I took pity on the Dutch Boy. Maybe I got lost in my own feelings of loneliness. Anyway, I decided this little couple would like to be reunited.

I proceeded outside and gave the little guy a good cleaning. I was able to get the dirt and mold off of him using a hard scrub brush. He would dry in the sun while I rounded up the supplies needed to spruce him up. After scrounging through my collection of odds-and-ends cans and bottles of paint, I found enough colors to give my Dutch Boy a fresh outfit. There was plenty of the blue paint I'd used for the girl's dress. With a basket loaded with all the containers of paint, brushes, tools, and cleanup items, I headed out to the back yard.

For a brief moment, I hesitated going forward with my project. Did my Dutch Boy deserve my time? He did have that clearly visible crack around his neck. When hosing him down, I'd notice how unsightly it was. Whoever glued his head back on hadn't done a very good job. Being on stay-at-home orders, there was no way to run to a store to get what was necessary to cover the crack.

Waiting wasn't an option! I knew if I didn't do it now, he'd probably never be painted. Besides, I had nothing better to do. So, I spread out the old sheet I was using for a drop cloth and lined up the different colors. The transformation began — the more I painted the more I smiled.

What joy it brought me to see him restored. His hat was now bright blue, matching his freshly painted pants. They looked perfect resting on his shiny black shoes. Once again, his hair was blonde and clean. The tulips he was hiding behind his back were popping with brilliant red blooms. Now, he was presentable enough to go see his partner.

For a change I'd thought ahead about how to move him across the yard. He didn't feel that heavy when I pulled him on the large piece of cardboard I'd rolled him onto. Once he was close enough, I carefully wobbled him back and forth till he stood a little way apart from the Dutch girl. I felt so good as I admired the happy couple — at last together again.

Of course, I took plenty of pictures! It made a cute story on Facebook explaining how they had to be socially distanced. During this pandemic, many were experiencing the disappointment of not being able to hug and kiss their loved ones. Maybe the couple, standing an arm's length apart and waiting to get close enough to kiss, would help others realize we were all feeling the pain of separation. Sometimes it can cheer us up just knowing we are not alone in our struggles.

As I got the two back together the Lord reminded me that we are all just broken pieces of clay — broken pottery. But He still desires to use us to bring others some happiness or joy. He doesn't wait until we are perfect, just as I didn't wait until I got some putty to cover the huge crack around the boy's neck. Instead, I accepted him just as he was. The broken and cracked Dutch boy made me realize no one is hopeless. I delighted myself in making something beautiful of him — in spite of his imperfections.

We all are broken in different ways. Some of us were injured in bad relationships. Perhaps, as we went through the healing process, it left us with some very obvious scars. Maybe those who attempted to put us back together didn't do such a great job. Our hurts may still be showing. Some of us may feel like we are that big gray glob of nothing. It's not true! No one is worthless. We are precious and have value even though we might look like a hot mess.

That evening I glanced out my kitchen window. The view was far enough away that I couldn't see the Dutch boy's brokenness. All I saw was the cute couple puckered up- waiting anxiously for the pandemic to be over. God is watching us but not necessarily from a distance. Although He is very aware of our cracks and missing pieces, He chooses not to make them His focus. Instead, He envisions us as what we can be.

If we will let Him, God can use us just as we are. My afternoon project turned into a sweet reminder from the Lord. He is the patient potter slowly molding us into well-formed vessels — constantly repainting our portraits. Jesus' blood covered our flaws just as if we got a new coat of paint. We are never so broken that He will discard us.

We *can* cheer someone up. We *can* make someone happy today! All it may take is a text, a phone call, or a card to let them know we care. I pray you are lifted up by the thought that God never gives up on us. If you are, pay it forward by encouraging someone else today!

I will praise thee; for I am fearfully and wonderfully made: marvellous are thy works; and that my soul knoweth right well.
(Psalm 139:14 KJV)

For we are his workmanship, created in Christ Jesus unto good works, which God hath before ordained that we should walk in them.
(Eph. 2:10 KJV)

Lesson Twenty-Four

Hidden Sin

He that covereth his sins shall not prosper: but whoso confesseth and forsaketh them shall have mercy.
(Prov. 28:13 KJV)

It was early spring—just warm enough to begin to tackle cleaning out the flower beds that decorated the edges of my backyard. My neighbor has a gigantic oak tree that shades both of our yards. Since oak trees are notorious for hanging on to their leaves, it is next to impossible to dispose of them all before winter sets in. Thus, the final clean-up never happens until the end of winter when the weather breaks. My leaf blower had plenty of power to clear out all the brown leftover leaves that were stuck amid the ground cover and in the bases of the bushes.

I worked hard at this project. It took hours. The flower beds now looked great—swept clean. Every last leaf, the small branches, and leftover nuts the squirrels chose not to hide, were bagged up ready to be put on the curb for pick up. Done—it made me smile. I took one more walk around the yard admiring my efforts. The purple crocuses were now visible. Hyacinths, daffodils, and a few tulips were breaking through the ground. I envisioned the bursts of color that would soon pop up along the back fence.

That evening the wind was fierce. I could hear it howling around the house. As I dozed off to sleep, I whispered a prayer for the Lord to keep all the trees around my house standing. The next morning, when I pulled back my kitchen curtains, my heart sank. My bottom lip stuck out as I gazed at my back yard covered with leaves and branches. Everything I'd worked on the day before was undone—what a mess. I was so discouraged! The limbs and sticks I could understand—the wind had brought them down. But why were so many leaves everywhere and in my back flower beds? Where did they come from? When I stepped out of my door, I got part of my answer.

The neighbor had never had her yard cleaned up last fall. I really couldn't complain about it. She is elderly and not able to do it herself. Her family never finished the job they had started so her leaves easily found their way into my yard.

But I still couldn't quite understand the huge mess in my back flower beds. It was still breezy as I walked toward the wire fence along the back edge of the property. It separated me from the school playground directly behind me. There were some huge pieces of plywood leaning against this fence; they were there when I moved in my house and I'd left them. A few stakes were in front of them to keep them from falling over. The one board was bouncing back and forth between the support and the fencing.

As I stood there looking, a gust of wind blew a bunch of leaves from behind the plywood. Aha, that's where they came from! Piles of leaves had been trapped behind the wood. The storm stirred things up—pushed what was hiding out into the open. The big brown leaves swirled everywhere, cluttering up my once-clean flower beds. I sighed. I was going to have to dig out all the debris behind the boards unless I wanted to deal with a new mess every time the winds got strong.

When I walked inside to get my leaf blower, the Lord reminded me of the things in our lives—things we think we have hidden away. It's easy to dress up the way we look on the outside. We make sure all the flaws that would be clearly visible to those around us are tucked in. Most of us have hidden faults, failures, and even sins. We've kept them behind a wall—barriers we've put up.

But life happens and suddenly something starts moving those walls. Storms have a way of bringing out our true character. Hiding our failures and imperfections will not make them disappear. Some things may have gone undetected through many seasons of our lives. But when shifts in our circumstances come, the pretty picture we've tried to paint of ourselves suddenly fades. The winds of change expose whatever we've covered up.

Trials and hard times bring our issues to the surface so we can deal with them rather than keeping them tucked away. I could no longer ignore the leaves piled behind that plywood. It was hard work and kind of smelled removing the rotting leaves. So also, once who we really are becomes obvious, we have to figure out how to tear down our walls and clean up what's behind them. Sometimes it stinks when we dig out the dirt. But it has to be done. Otherwise, the issues we've never dealt with will continue to create messes.

Unfortunately, some of us try to build a higher fence. We can never build a wall high enough that God can't see behind. Eventually, a big enough storm will blow through and expose what is trapped behind our false smiles. We should thank God for those storms. Perhaps He sent one to help us see where we are stuck. It can be painful to admit we are struggling with certain problems. But acknowledgement is always the first step to healing. Once He shows us the truth, we need to be willing to get free.

I pray you look deep inside. Begin the process by clearing out some of your not-so-healthy mindsets. Face whatever you've buried, such as addictions, insecurity, bitterness, unforgiveness. Ask the Lord to give you strategies for getting rid of those hidden issues. You'll feel so good once you clean it all up! Find your freedom today!

And ye shall know the truth, and the truth shall make you free.
(John 8:32 KJV)

For every one that doeth evil hateth the light, neither cometh to the light, lest his deeds should be reproved. But he that doeth truth cometh to the light, that his deeds may be made manifest, that they are wrought in God.
(John 3:20-21 KJV)

Lesson Twenty-Five

My Ugly Oak Tree

Let the wicked forsake his way, and the unrighteous man his thoughts: and let him return unto the Lord, and he will have mercy upon him; and to our God, for he will abundantly pardon.
(Is. 55:7 KJV)

The view from my big picture window is lovely. No houses across the street — just trees. There's a steep embankment and a winding river far below. I especially love how it looks when the trees are adorned with their leaves. As I gaze out my window, I can also see the young oak the city planted in the tree lawn in front of my house. In the summer I don't mind it but the rest of year I refer to it as my "ugly oak tree".

Although most oak trees retain their leaves far into the fall season, I've never seen one as stubborn as this one. As I lift my blinds every morning there it is. It's now mid-February and it's still full of huge, drooping, brown, dead leaves. They've lingered despite several severe winter storms with high velocity winds. It might not even be so bad if oak leaves were a mixture of brilliant colors; but they're not — they're just brown. I hate it! There is no other way to describe my tree. It is absolutely ugly.

This spring, when everything is bursting forth with new life, the old leaves will still be clinging to the tips of the branches. Some will even stay on after the new foliage appears. It is unbelievable how they could remain attached. Last year I pulled off the old ones but this year the tree is much taller and it kept far more leaves. I will not be able to reach them all. Already, I am despising how I imagine it will look this summer! The only way I can think of, to remedy this situation is to cut down this eyesore.

Staring at my oak this morning, I was reminded of how we sometimes refuse to let go of certain things in our lives. I tried to recall some of the stuff God has asked me to release. Then, the thought I had scared me. *"What does the Lord see when looking out the window of heaven? Is He pleased or am I an ugly oak tree in His garden?"*

Fortunately, God doesn't think like we do. I remembered the many seasons in my life when I was a huge disappointment to my Creator. And yet here I am, still standing and attempting to do His will. He didn't give up on me. What a relief! I serve a gracious God. He is full of mercy and longsuffering — not willing that any should perish.

We've all had times when we've hung onto people or characteristics that clearly make us look bad. Thankfully, the Lord makes every attempt possible to clean us up. He sends storms to blow the ugliness off. Even though we may not look like we want to now — just wait. He will do whatever is necessary to get us to loosen the grip on whatever is holding us back.

God isn't in the process of sharpening an ax to cut us down as I wanted to do to my tree. But at some point, He expects us to pay attention to His promptings and get rid of unnecessary stuff. Some of us continue in toxic relationships even though we know a certain person is not good for us. Our family, our friends, and God, have warned us—advising us to leave. Unhealthy relationships are more obvious to those who are observing them from the outside. Others can usually see when we are being used or abused and it is not a pretty sight to them. We should listen to good, sound advice and begin the process of letting go. Maybe it's time to shake off those who are keeping us from blossoming. Is there someone hindering you from becoming the beautiful person God intends you to be?

An individual doesn't have to be bad or evil for us to separate from them. It just may be time to move forward. Maybe they were in your life for a season and the Lord has a change for you that doesn't include them. We can't always take everyone with us. Cut the ties if God has asked.

Letting go isn't only about people. Perhaps the Lord is asking you to change physical locations but you can't quite walk away from a house you've become attached to. Put it on the market. Things we put too much value on are just like those unsightly brown leaves on my tree.

God may be sending the wind of His Spirit to free us from some of our possessions. Having a lot of stuff may not be sin. But when we become preoccupied with acquiring an abundance of whatever, it can interfere with us seeking after spiritual things. The Bible tells us where our treasure is, there will our hearts be also.

Also, we sometimes can be stubborn and hold onto activities we like to do. Life has many distractions. In order to develop a close relationship with the Lord, we have to be aware of where our focus is. If our eyes are on some entertainment or recreation that consumes most of our time, it can hinder us from finding out our true purpose in life. Maybe we just need to put down the phone, stop playing the video game, or turn off the computer and the television. Once we set aside a special time for Him, it will be much easier to develop a closeness with Him. Listen for the winds of change. Let them blow away whatever it is we think we cannot live without.

When we allow anything to hang around long enough, we get comfortable with it. It becomes a part of our lifestyle. The longer we do things in a certain way with certain people the harder it is to change. When doing something different becomes too difficult—we're stuck. It's just like my tree. This year I'm not even sure new buds will be able to knock off the old leaves on my tree—they're stuck like glue.

It is up to us to find out what has our total attention. If our security rests in something other than the Lord, there may be a problem. First, identify what our anchor is. Have we latched onto something besides God to feel safe? Second, admit we have placed our hope in a person or in things instead of God. Finally, do what my leaves refuse to do—let it go.

The saying "Live, Love, and Laugh" seems to be a formula for maintaining a good life. I think we should add "Let Go" to that list. My prayer is for us to stop allowing our beauty to be marred by hanging onto someone or something. May we cling to Jesus for dear life. When we hold onto Him, it will be easy to loosen the grip on whatever is hindering us from moving forward.

I'm sure God wonders why it takes us so long to get rid of some of our stuff. Perhaps, He's even shaking His head saying, "Do they realize how totally unattractive they are?" Today, I am so grateful our God is full of mercy and grace. Instead of contemplating cutting us down, He continually tries to show us how to get rid of whatever detracts from our beauty. We may not be as pretty as we think!

What are you hanging on to? Do yourself a favor! Release it to God! Then you can find your peace and inner beauty as you bud out with new growth.

Therefore if any man be in Christ, he is a new creature: old things are passed away; behold, all things are become new.
(2 Cor. 5:17 KJV)

That ye put off concerning the former conversation the old man, which is corrupt according to the deceitful lusts; And be renewed in the spirit of your mind; And that ye put on the new man, which after God is created in righteousness and true holiness.
(Eph. 4:22-24 KJV)

Lesson Twenty-Six

Praise Him in the Storm

Blessed be the King that cometh in the name of the Lord: peace in heaven, and glory in the highest. And some of the Pharisees from among the multitude said unto him, Master, rebuke thy disciples. And he answered and said unto them, I tell you that, if these should hold their peace, the stones would immediately cry out.
(Luke 38:40 KJV)

I stared out my window at the branches of my lilac bushes and smaller trees. They were bent over — touching the ground from the weight of the snow. It was unusual to get twelve plus inches of heavy snow in my hometown. This had been quite a winter storm. They'd warned us it was coming so I'd already called off from work- happy I didn't have to go anywhere! From the inside looking out, still snuggled in my pajamas, I could thoroughly enjoy the beauty of my backyard winter wonderland.

As I looked out at this spectacular picture of the snow, my thoughts went to the Lord. The branches seemed to be bowing down before the Creator. It was like they were worshipping

Him. The scriptures came to mind about the rocks praising Him if we don't.

I began to praise the Lord for His goodness. There I was, safe and warm in my home and I hadn't lost power. Due to high winds and significant snowfall, branches had fallen on wires in many places causing outages in nearby neighborhoods. Also, I was grateful my daughter was able to navigate her car back to her house. Earlier, she'd made an attempt to go to work. After initially getting stuck in her drive, she was able to get onto the road where her car began fish-tailing. That's when she turned around and made it safely back home. This day, the Lord gently reminded me I had lots to praise Him for in the storm. I certainly didn't want a rock or a branch to do my worshipping for me.

My son-in-law shoveled out my driveway later that day — not that I was going to be leaving the house. The following day, he removed the few extra inches that had fallen after the fact. The brightly shining sun was a welcome sight as it beat down on my steep driveway melting the small telltale spots of snow. Eventually, I ventured out to clean off my car. That was a lot of work — over a foot of snow isn't that easy to move.

This was sort of an odd storm in that it was a one-day event. Twenty-four hours later the temperature would take a huge jump up. So, it was unbelievable how swiftly the thaw took place. The once heavily-laden branches of the bushes and trees were beginning to bounce back as the snow began falling off. Some popped right up with a quick jerk. Other more mature ones, carried more of the weight of the snow. The larger amounts were taking longer to melt, so those branches were slower to move back to their upright positions.

Watching this turned into another lesson for me. After our storms in life, we all go through a recovery process. When we are young with our whole life ahead of us, we sometimes bounce back quicker than the older generation. That's one of the joys of being a child. In the innocence of youth, we do not always realize the seriousness of situations. Thus, we don't carry the weight of not knowing the next step to take in the middle of a crisis. The adults, those who are more mature, are the ones who bear the bigger burdens—just like the big branches held more snow.

The older we are it seems like the responsibility of figuring out solutions during difficult times falls on us. The stress of it all can take a toll. There will be times when our burdens are so tremendous that we break under the pressure. One of my neighbor's bushes had a big branch that snapped right off. It couldn't withstand the weight of the snow. Its problem was that it couldn't bend. We need to remain pliable by looking for the good, even in the bad times. Then, try to find a praise in the midst of hardships. Worshiping God may be exactly what keeps us from losing control. We are never too mature or too important to refuse to bow down to our Creator. Do it even when life doesn't feel good.

I am certain Paul and Silas weren't comfortable in prison. The Bible tells us they sang praises while they were locked in stocks. They proved miracles can happen in impossible situations. God's servant, Job, is another example of being able to worship the Lord after suffering tremendous losses. In our worst situations, praise might very well be the key to bring about the changes we are looking for.

You may be weathering a huge storm in your life right now. Maybe your circumstances have completely changed —

suddenly everything stable has been turned upside-down. As adults, we face difficult spiritual battles when unforeseen things happen. The struggle is real as we attempt to get a handle on situations just to survive daily. Be aware, we are never going it alone. The Lord is in our corner as we learn to cope in adverse times. It may be too big of a problem for us to fix; but nothing is impossible to God.

Storms are temporary—the sun will shine again. It did the day after the snowstorm and I watched the branches rising up. Some did quickly and for others the recovery process was a gradual one. We should be patient and choose to praise the Lord as we emerge from all our storms. After they are over, we too can be standing with our heads held high.

Just as I watched the trees and bushes bounce back from my window, God is watching us. He is right by our side allowing the "Son" to shine on us. Be encouraged today as we walk through every situation—especially the ones we thought would crush us. Tomorrow is only a day away! The Lord has already prepared all we will need for whatever May come our way in the future. As we step into each tomorrow, keep our focus on eternal things. That will help us to remember one of God's special promises. The bible tells us there will come a day when we will not have to face any more storms ever.

And God shall wipe away all tears from their eyes; and there shall be no more death, neither sorrow, nor crying, neither shall there be any more pain: for the former things are passed away. And he that sat upon the throne said, Behold, I make all things new. And he

said unto me, Write: for these words are true and faithful.
(Rev. 21:4-5 KJV)

I will bless the Lord at all times: his praise shall continually be in my mouth.
(Psalm 34:1 KJV)

Scriptures about Paul and Silas and Job can be found printed in the back of this book.

Scriptures and Prayers Referenced in Some of the Devotionals

For your convenience, I have printed a few of the Bible stories I referenced in this book. All of these scriptures are from the King James Version. I've also included a prayer you may like to read to help you on your journey.

Lesson Two – The Lord is My Shepherd

The 23rd Psalm

The Lord is my shepherd; I shall not want. He maketh me to lie down in green pastures: he leadeth me beside the still waters. He restoreth my soul: he leadeth me in the paths of righteousness for his name's sake. Yea, though I walk through the valley of the shadow of death, I will fear no evil: for thou art with me; thy rod and thy staff they comfort me. Thou preparest a table before me in the presence of mine enemies: thou anointest my head with oil; my cup runneth over. Surely goodness and mercy shall follow me all the days of my life: and I will dwell in the house of the Lord for ever.

Lesson Three – Swinging on Grapevines

The Pharisee and the Publican – Luke 18:9-14

And he spake this parable unto certain which trusted in themselves that they were righteous, and despised others: Two men went up into the temple to pray; the one a Pharisee, and the other a publican. The Pharisee stood and prayed thus with himself, God, I thank thee, that I am not as other men are, extortioners, unjust, adulterers, or even as this publican. I fast twice in the week, I give tithes of all that I possess. And the publican, standing afar off, would not lift up so much as his eyes unto heaven, but smote upon his breast, saying, God be merciful to me a sinner. I tell you, this man went down to his house justified rather than the other: for every one that exalteth himself shall be abased; and he that humbleth himself shall be exalted.

The Good Samaritan – Luke 10:25-37

And, behold, a certain lawyer stood up, and tempted him, saying, Master, what shall I do to inherit eternal life? He said unto him, What is written in the law? how readest thou? And he answering said, Thou shalt love the Lord thy God with all thy heart, and with all thy soul, and with all thy strength, and with all thy mind; and thy neighbour as thyself. And he said unto him, Thou hast answered right: this do, and thou shalt live.

But he, willing to justify himself, said unto Jesus, And who is my neighbour?

And Jesus answering said, A certain man went down from Jerusalem to Jericho, and fell among thieves, which stripped him of his raiment, and wounded him, and departed, leaving him half dead. And by chance there came down a certain priest that way: and when he saw him, he passed by on the other side. And likewise a Levite, when he was at the place, came and looked on him, and passed by on the other side.

But a certain Samaritan, as he journeyed, came where he was: and when he saw him, he had compassion on him, And went to him, and bound up his wounds, pouring in oil and wine, and set him on his own beast, and brought him to an inn, and took care of him. And on the morrow when he departed, he took out two pence, and gave them to the host, and said unto him, Take care of him; and whatsoever thou spendest more, when I come again, I will repay thee. Which now of these three, thinkest thou, was neighbour unto him that fell among the thieves? And he said, He that shewed mercy on him. Then said Jesus unto him, Go, and do thou likewise.

Lesson Four – Cracking Open Rocks

Jesus calling out the scribes and Pharisees – Matt. 23:27

Woe unto you, scribes and Pharisees, hypocrites! for ye are like unto whited sepulchres, which indeed appear beautiful outward, but are within full of dead men's bones, and of all uncleanness.

Lesson Eight — My Fairy Godmother

A Prayer to Accept Jesus as Your Ticket to Heaven

Jesus, I come to you today admitting I have failed and sinned against you. I acknowledge you have paid the price for all of sins by your death on the cross. Please forgive me for everything I have done, said, or thought wrong. Come into my heart and teach me how to live right. I make you the Lord, the Prince of my life – In Jesus Name – Amen!

Lesson Nine - The Cream of the Crop

Peter's denial – Luke 22:54-62

Then took they him, and led him, and brought him into the high priest's house. And Peter followed afar off. And when they had kindled a fire in the midst of the hall, and were set down together, Peter sat down among them. But a certain maid beheld him as he sat by the fire, and earnestly looked upon him, and said, This man was also with him. And he denied him, saying, Woman, I know him not. And after a little while another saw him, and said, Thou art also of them. And Peter said, Man, I am not. And about the space of one hour after another confidently affirmed, saying, Of a truth this fellow also was with him: for he is a Galilaean. And Peter said, Man, I know not what thou sayest. And immediately, while he yet spake, the cock crew. And the Lord turned, and looked upon Peter. And Peter remembered the word of the Lord, how he had said unto him, Before the cock crow, thou shalt deny me thrice. And Peter went out, and wept bitterly.

Lesson Ten - Under Pressure

Shadrach, Meshach, and Abednego — Dan. 3:16-27

Shadrach, Meshach, and Abednego, answered and said to the king, O Nebuchadnezzar, we are not careful to answer thee in this matter. If it be so, our God whom we serve is able to deliver us from the burning fiery furnace, and he will deliver us out of thine hand, O king. But if not, be it known unto thee, O king, that we will not serve thy gods, nor worship the golden image which thou hast set up. Then was Nebuchadnezzar full of fury, and the form of his visage was changed against Shadrach, Meshach, and Abednego: therefore he spake, and commanded that they should heat the furnace one seven times more than it was wont to be heated. And he commanded the most mighty men that were in his army to bind Shadrach, Meshach, and Abednego, and to cast them into the burning fiery furnace. Then these men were bound in their coats, their hosen, and their hats, and their other garments, and were cast into the midst of the burning fiery furnace. Therefore because the king's commandment was urgent, and the furnace exceeding hot, the flames of the fire slew those men that took up Shadrach, Meshach, and Abednego. And these three men, Shadrach, Meshach, and Abednego, fell down bound into the midst of the burning fiery furnace. Then Nebuchadnezzar the king was astonished, and rose up in haste, and spake, and said unto his counsellors, Did not we cast three men bound into the midst of the fire? They answered and said unto the king, True, O king. He answered and said, Lo, I see four men loose, walking in the midst of the fire, and they have no hurt; and the form of the fourth is like the Son of God. Then Nebuchadnezzar came near to the mouth of the burning fiery furnace, and spake, and said, Shadrach, Meshach, and Abednego, ye servants of the most high God, come forth, and come hither. Then Shadrach, Meshach, and Abednego, came forth of the midst of the fire. And the princes, governors, and captains, and the king's counsellors, being gathered together, saw these men, upon whose bodies the fire had no power, nor was an hair of their head singed, neither were their coats changed, nor the smell of fire had passed on them.

Lesson Seventeen - Flow Like a River

The Vine – John 5:1-5

I am the true vine, and my Father is the husbandman. Every branch in me that beareth not fruit he taketh away: and every branch that beareth fruit, he purgeth it, that it may bring forth more fruit. Now ye are clean through the word which I have spoken unto you. Abide in me, and I in you. As the branch cannot bear fruit of itself, except it abide in the vine; no more can ye, except ye abide in me. I am the vine, ye are the branches: He that abideth in me, and I in him, the same bringeth forth much fruit: for without me ye can do nothing.

Lesson Twenty-Six – Praise Him in the Storm

Paul and Silas – Acts 16:25-26

And at midnight Paul and Silas prayed, and sang praises unto God: and the prisoners heard them. And suddenly there was a great earthquake, so that the foundations of the prison were shaken: and immediately all the doors were opened, and every one's bands were loosed.

Job – Job 1:20-22

Then Job arose, and rent his mantle, and shaved his head, and fell down upon the ground, and worshipped, And said, Naked came I out of my mother's womb, and naked shall I return thither: the Lord gave, and the Lord hath taken away; blessed be the name of the Lord. In all this Job sinned not, nor charged God foolishly.

Made in United States
Cleveland, OH
28 September 2025